Copyright © 2022 Leo X. Robertson

A Planet Bizarro publication. All rights reserved.

The characters and events portrayed in this book are fictitious. Any similarity to actual persons, living or dead, is coincidental and not intended by the author.

No part of this book may be reproduced, or stored in a retrieval system, or transmitted in any form or by any means, electronic, mechanical, photocopying, recording, or otherwise, without express written permission of the publisher.

Edited by Matthew A. Clarke

Cover by Adrian Medina

Weird Fauna of the Multiverse

Leo X. Robertson

Planet Bizarro Press

CONTENTS

1. Koalita, Mon Amour — 1
2. Chapter One — 4
3. Chapter Two — 12
4. Chapter Three — 16
5. Chapter Four — 23
6. Chapter Five — 29
7. Chapter Six — 34
8. Chapter Seven — 38
9. Chapter Eight — 42
10. Chapter Nine — 49
11. Chapter Ten — 54
12. Chapter Eleven — 61
13. Chapter Twelve — 65
14. Dinosaurs of the CyberVatican: — 68
15. Chapter Two — 79

16.	Chapter Three	87
17.	Chapter Four	93
18.	Chapter Five	95
19.	Chapter Six	99
20.	Chapter Seven	101
21.	Chapter Eight	103
22.	Everybody Wants to Save	106
23.	Chapter Two	113
24.	Chapter Three	121
25.	Chapter Four	131
26.	Chapter Five	145

About the Author 147

Afterword 148

New and Upcoming from Planet Bizarro 150

KOALITA, MON AMOUR

INTRODUCTION: THE FALL OF KOALATOPIA

The year was 3945. The planet, Venus.

Dis, the leader of the koalas, indulged in a celebratory orgy with his hundred or so marsupial concubines. They lay together beneath the plentiful sun of early afternoon on Lower Venus. Koalas slipped off their togas and tossed them aside. They pleasured one another with saturnalian glee. When changing position or partner, they passed around eucalyptus spliffs or small brown vials of the plant's oil. The vials shone in the sunlight as koalas thrusted the bottles between their partners for aphrodisiacal insufflation.

The temple—upon which Dis and his followers pawed appendages, nibbled teats and poked pockets—was the hemisphere's pride. It was a dome carved from a single block of rose stone. A feeling of absolute safety permeated this utopian community as they copulated without a care on the temple's roof, in the open air. Beneath the dome were many other species available for carnal delights, humans especially, but today's midday fuckfest was a koala exclusive, a special celebration.

For reasons unknown, an infinite series of two-dimensional universes had sliced through Venus and elongated its ball shape into a disembodied, semi-erect penis. This separated the koalas from Upper Venus for good, dislocating them from the danger of the lava giants who lived there. They called this The Great Separation.

When Dis was spent, he lay on the warm stone and looked at the sky. A glowing portal had opened above the temple. It wobbled like a mercury mirror, reflecting the blinding sun for most of the day. When Dis squinted at it through his sunglasses, he swore he could see the glass trees of Upper Venus. The portal was some sort of transportation device. The koalas hadn't the technology to reach it, nor the desire to do so anyway.

A black disc popped out of the portal. As Dis stood up, staring at the object, it expanded to frisbee size. Soon it was big enough to take over the sun.

A eucalyptus leaf dropped from Dis' lower lip. He signaled to the other koalas. They parted from their various copulating configurations to join him in staring upwards at the device. As it lowered towards them, they huddled together, gathering at one side of the roof's plateau like a furry pupil to the temple's eye.

The disc was a UFO. A slice fell out of it, making a walkway as it landed. A large hippo strutted out and onto the sunbaked stone, a white space suit hugging his portly shape.

He spoke with a honeyed voice. "My dearest marsupial brethren, please don't let me interrupt."

A mist of hippo wetness sizzled off his face, evaporating into the Venusian air.

Dis stepped forward, maintaining as much dignity about him as he could while shuffling his toga back on. "I am Dis Koalawannaleya, leader of Lower Venus." He eyed up the hippo. "What can we do you for? Five euros?"

The hippo tittered.

An ocelot slinked out of the UFO and slumped in its shadow, glaring at the koalas with menace.

A giraffe trotted out and tried to hide behind the hippo, to no avail. He hissed at his hooves as they clopped loudly on the temple's surface.

A dray of squirrels scurried out next, slithering across the stone and between the koalas, with chipper curiosity. The koalas parted from one another and batted at the squirrels with ashamed paws, thinking it wise not to protest more strongly—because the supercilious simper on the hippo's face told them something bad was coming.

The hippo clasped his forefeet behind his back. "Mr Koalawannaleya, I'll abstain from your generous offer of fraternization."

Dis pressed a paw to his heart. The way the hippo had spat the word "fraternization": Surely he wasn't—

"Boris Hippoman himself, in the thick and plentiful flesh."

Dis held his arms out as if to shield the hundred-odd koalas behind him. "What do you want with us?"

Boris clapped his paws together, suit crinkling with the gesture. "I'm here to take you back to Upper Venus' glass forest."

The koalas murmured with dissatisfaction.

Dis raised a paw in protest. "Never! So many of us crisped, burned and melted when we escaped to Lower Venus. We won't go back. I won't have it!"

The year previous, beleaguered koalas had made a pilgrimage out of Upper Venus' glass forest. Lava giants had spewed from volcanos and begun a bloody subjugation of all animals who sought to oppose them. The koalas reached Lower Venus and made a haven following The Great Separation. They used the tragedy of home-fleeing as fuel for lives of hedonistic pleasure. Dis had commissioned the temple in honour of this.

Boris raised a forefoot. It made a snapping sound somehow, as if he'd had fingers and clicked them. "You won't go back to Upper Venus the easy way, you mean."

The ocelot scampered back to the UFO. A whirring sound emanated from beneath the sleek metal panels. Cannons emerged from the disc's edge.

Nets of extra-terrestrial effluvium shot out and snagged the koalas with ease, sticking to their fur. They milled around beneath it in a brown carpet of distress.

Dis skidded across the ground. The force of the net smashed his sunglasses.

The shock of it got the squirrels to dissipate. They slipped easily through holes in the net and returned to the UFO.

Boris' laugh was low and gravelly as he turned his back to the koalas, securing their net to a hook at the UFO's base. He took the walkway back in, and the UFO closed.

A metallic voice spoke from some unseen loudspeaker, its inorganic resonance shivering through the terrified curio of koalas: "Hold your breath now," it said, "but don't worry! Not long until we reach Ecofallopialand."

CHAPTER ONE

Exhausted, the body of Sir marched on all fours.

The intelligent solar tiling beneath him sang alarms of warning about the dangers of spending prolonged periods on one's knees.

"Believe me, he knows," Mistress said, flicking her Bettie Page-style hair over one shoulder.

A guard in formal gear held up a flaccid screwdriver and whispered an apology. "We forgot to configure these panels for the event."

It was Gimp Week on Ecofallopialand, and Sir was far from the only chap staggering about the place so close to the ground. However, he was the only gimp whose fetish gear sported gold-plated leather and diamond spikes. These adornments compromised the material's suppleness. Strips of it shuffled awkwardly and almost of their own accord between the rings of platinum that held each rib-like component together. The muzzle and dog ears collected Sir's hot breath and sweat.

To Mistress' dismay, Sir's weighty, rectally inserted tailpiece swivelled and drooped. The metal ball of its interior acted like a heat conductor, slowly simmering his bowels. She made sure to add, to his nightly list, exercise reps for the skeletal muscle of his overly peg-sodomized anus. She liked a pup with perk, but this one was peakish and scalding to the touch.

Above them, a tree of tempered glass stretched to the tip of Venus' dense, carbonaceous atmosphere. A glowing screen inside displayed, upon its shield, an array of marauding, bruise-dark clouds that barreled around in an upside-down funnel shape like an inverse tornado at quarter-speed. Torrential rains of sulfuric acid were visible at a squint. They fuzzed the milky glass, but its shield kept out every drop. It also maintained its internals' pressure and gaseous content, which depended on the visitor's species—humans only, this week—but regulated temperature poorly.

To Sir, Venus' roiling, boiling exterior exerted a frightening heat.

The other gimps' leather wilted. Sir crawled over one in front of him who had hopefully only passed out—though the smell of his baking body indicated death.

Evening would soon be upon the leathered lovers. They'd spent the morning on an airboat in The Earth That Time Forgot, speeding across the slime lagoon-machine's waters. The exhibit simulated Earth's conditions way back in 2166. In the afternoon, Mistress had bought Sir a funnel spider cake in the Abominated Aviary. Criminals convicted of only the worst Intersolar crimes flapped, with wings of corpsemeat, a precarious distance beneath an egg-shaped electrified cage. The slightest touch would fry them like zapped blue bottles. The cage's heavy buzzing caused the criminals' noses to bleed in continuous tar-like streams that they licked at with tired tongues through dry lips. Beneath them was one of the planet's many pores. The wings would eventually slough off them through the rotting process, and the pore would suck them in, send them down Venus' burning core.

The day wound down, and they'd reached their last stop: The Surviving Outback. Men with specially painted harnesses got their "Ayers Rocks off!" pretending to be kangaroos. The joeys in their front pockets were often real and struggling to escape: post-embryonic beans of pink dragged around cold human bellies in search of maternal, marsupial warmth, failing and perishing in the pursuit. Some men appropriated traditional aboriginal designs for the near-blasphemous purpose of pretending to be a didgeridoo. They lay in the hot, Australia-imported dirt and invited guests to fellate them. During this act, they burbled and growled, mimicking the sound of air resonating through a wooden pipe.

"Look, darling slave." Mistress walked Sir above the land, across a segmented bridge of enlarged glass wallaby vertebrae. She unscrewed a telescope from his tail and flicked it out, directing her attention to an ersatz eucalyptus tree, on which, from their distance, brown mites seemed to dance.

Sir perked up. "I have permission?"

Mistress nodded.

He accepted the telescope and looked through it. In the distance was a collection of koalas with groggy, salivating mouths and eucalyptus pulp stuck on their gums. They wailed in delight, too far away to hear properly, little paws flailing without a care, all behaving like this—except one.

"Wow."

Sir's koala of interest leaned in a sultry manner along a thick branch, her chocolate fur matching the hue of its bark.

"See something you like?" Mistress' tone implied a generous mother inviting a child to show her a toy he'd been hankering for. This mood evaporated as she pointed the telescope where he'd looked and saw the mysterious eyes of a koala slut looking back at her. She tutted.

Sir pawed at her leg like a good pup. "Can we get a picture taken with it?"

Mistress reached between her breasts and produced a riding crop she'd earlier tucked neatly into her corset. With it, she whipped him across the cheek, cutting his face. "Look at that second mouth!" She passed the telescope back to him.

From the side of a creature's abdomen, he observed a mouth extending from rib to hip. It flapped as the little koala lady shimmied around.

"See the lips on it? They're usually black. This one has red lips. She has koalamydia."

"Sweet lemony koala pussy," Sir said.

"No need to use the safe words! I barely scratched your face. Maybe *you're* the koala pussy."

"To your point though, since when have koalas had second mouths on—"

"Spare me, pig! No one in this millennium needs koala evolution explained. Next, you're gonna remind me about the time when human women had assholes."

A grappling hook swung around the vertebra in front of them, looping twice around and snagging on its own attached rope.

"Hello, you two!" A gangly zookeeper scrambled up the rope. He wore an outback hat, cargo shorts and a T-shirt embroidered with the park's logo: *Ecofallopialand* in cartoon intestine lettering.

Sir and Mistress helped him up.

"Your dominatrix here has quite astutely observed an issue of prime concern here in the zoo. We no longer allow patrons to take photos with our koalas. Why, even the lustiest koala fetishists know not to break the rules."

He pointed. Like butter gliding in a pan, distant objects shone through the wavy heat.

Sir looked at them with the telescope. Near the koalas—in branded plastic tents available at all good nearby retailers of memorabilic tat—tar-slicked men coated in fur, of questionable origin, hotboxed themselves with eucalyptus bongs and clawed at the clear plastic, their nails like "Weow, weow, weow!"

The zookeeper spoke again. "Remember a time of toilet seats, the source of one hundred percent of new herpes infections in humans? A time of hugging, the only source of scabies transference? A time of using your scabby flatmate's dirty towel, the only possible way you woke up with his pubic lice? If you believe all self-assessments. Humans used to engage in many activities with deleterious effects that we learned from and discontinued. Next on the list is koala contact. Koalamydia will make you whoop like a gibbon, poop a white ribbon and shoot hoops like, uh—Michael Jordan."

Mistress bowed to him. "Thank you for being so informative, Mr Zookeeper. Froot Loops?"

"That's a given."

She held out her hand to feed him Froot Loops.

Sir laughed.

"Something funny, fucker?!" Mistress said.

"Has there been no better basketball player since Michael Jordan?"

"Not that I'd know of," the zookeeper said. "Don't mock my references!"

"AHHH!!"

"What's that?" Sir said.

The zookeeper held out a calming hand. "The Screaming Eyeballs of Sleep."

A swarm of beach ball-sized eyeballs filled the sky. They split along their centres to open their mouths: "AAHHH!!"

All parkgoers lay down where they stood, the gentle yelling soon lulling the crew to sleep.

A park-wide net, connected to winches all up the side of the glass tree, rose from the floor and selectively snagged only the visitors. The nearby hotel, the shape and texture of a city-sized echidna's four-headed wang, split open along its base and inverted. Guests got poured into this spongy, bleeding opening. They barreled down its branches and landed in the nearest empty room. The penis inverted and re-sealed itself to the ground to clot overnight and heal, rings of shiny scar tissue indicating hundreds of such performances over the years.

In the middle of the night, Sir and Mistress rose with thirst, approaching the feeders by the door and lapping at the steel balls in their tubes to release a flow of water.

"You're up," Mistress said.

"About today—"

"Forget that. You need to perform your nightly exercises to stay in shape for tomorrow. Open the suitcase and you'll find your equipment."

Sir pulled a suitcase out from beneath the bed. Inside were plastic shopping bags filled with dirt, attached to bungee cords. He looped the cords over the frame of wood connecting the four posts of the bed and wrapped the free ends of them around his hands. There he stood, naked, tugging on the cords, dragging the dirtbags up, opposing Venus' epic gravitational resistance.

Some hours into this activity, as the sky turned a sombre ochre, he saw two tiny pinpricks of light at the window.

Could it be?

Upon approach, the pinpricks—the eyes and their owner—skittered away.

"How did you get out?" Sir whispered to the fleeing figure.

Mistress stirred. "Hm?"

Sir turned to her. "N-Nothing."

"Go to your bed. You've done enough for the night."

While curled up on newspaper in the room's corner, dreams revealed to Sir his true intent, his marsupiosexual awakening.

She appeared to him, his red-lipped beauty, through a trailing purple mist reminiscent of the synthetic sky's clouds. She wore a tutu of diaphanous pink crepe paper, which she pawed at coyly, her clear desire that Sir rip the frilly thing right off her.

He would oblige in time—but first, he reached a hand out.

Hand-painted eucalyptus leaves of every colour fell around them, some gathering softly in his palm.

She leaned forwards, paw covering her mouth with the timidity of a Japanese schoolgirl, hiding her incisor-nibbling of the leaves in his hand.

With one jerk, he reached forwards and grabbed her chin.

She gasped but let the hand linger there.

His other hand reached out. He ran the backs of his fingers through the tufts of her ears as the chocolate dollops of her beady eyes peered at him with lascivious curiosity.

Hands slid around her waist, one arm running through the cavernous mouth of human dentition which occupied her left side. He felt the heat of its yearning breath, the roughness of its tongue lapping wetly at his arm.

She leaned to one side to bring down the teeth on that arm, applying gentle but dangerous pressure.

The heat of those inflamed lips coaxed his erection to full mast. He lay down, and she positioned herself over his impressive member. His skin turned downy, brown fur coating his surface like soft grass creeping from wholesome soil. His newly grown vestigial tail assisted his thrust into the home of his true pleasure.

From an Ecofallopialand plaque in The Surviving Outback region.

Genetic engineers invented koalas in the mid-1990s—by accident.

This is according to a series of incomplete scientific records retrieved from Earth, the supposed home planet of humans.

The globalist government commissioned The Committee of Dumb Animals to produce a more rudimentary human form. They sought to do this using a mixture of caveman and lobster DNA.

Experts hypothesized the following properties of the resulting creature:

1. Docile, easily impressionable mind, free from delusions of grandeur.

2. Knows its place in society and stays there (i.e. ranking highly on Korsakoff's infamous enslavability index.)

3. Susceptible to commonly available psychotropic drugs.

These can thus be utilized as a cheap reward for menial labour.

Imagine the scientists' frustration when this process resulted in Philip "Sparky" Bugnuggets, the very first koala!

Sparky was a lazy marsupial who spent his days engorged on eucalyptus plants and had no desire to perform work of any kind.

As you can imagine, however, it wasn't long before the chief scientist, Veronica Seltzer, became endeared by Sparky's comical appearance and lovable personality.

A dilemma ensued. Sparky couldn't fulfil his original "rudimentary human" purpose. Plus, were the government to find out about him, they would surely issue an order to destroy him—and, by proxy, Seltzer's reputation. She had no room for error as a female working in a STEM field and heiress to the Seltzer family fortune.

Luckily, she had a brother who worked in marketing, Philharmonic Seltzer. Together they rebranded the koala as a sort of amusement device. One can easily imagine the comical appearance entertaining the courtesans of that era!

From a type of audio portraiture of this era, recorded onto "compact discs", we learned that "rappers" lorded over Earth's kingdoms, adorning themselves with heavy gold jewellery. During daily prayer sessions, a rapper would take to his tower with a megaphone and give spoken word performances of his courageous and bloody feats on the battlefields. His people would reward him with many virgins, dried dates and—greatest of honours—white snuffs. Scarce in supply, only aristocrats could insufflate these. They were otherwise used by international banks to back their various currencies.

Soon came the day that Veronica presented Sparky to her peninsula's rapper, Ice Cube, in Cube's opulently decorated chambers. The checkered floor's panels contained platinum and gold long-playing records coated in plastic resin. Pimp cups operated as light fixtures, filled with an eternally burning supply of Hennessy whisky. Velvet-covered footstools were scattered across the room to provide comfort for thick-thighed ladies.

Records show that Cube was initially enraged by the sight of Sparky, laughing with his ever-present entourage and openly mocking the beast. But the koala took out his three legendary test tubes and uttered his famous words: "Fancy a juggling treat?"

What historians would do for an image of Ice Cube's expression upon hearing this!

Sparky's intoxication prohibited a reasonable reaction time for juggling capability. He let the three test tubes smash to the floor.

Groupies, castrati and lesser rappers looked on in awe and disgust.

Cube laughed, the tension in the room vanished, and the koalas became the era's most popular derision-based entertainment.

To this day, we see the test tube and ice cube motif in tapestries on the cover of handbound books and paper plates from this time.

Want to learn more? Think very hard about it and one of Ecofallopialand's telepath staff will contact you with additional facts!

CHAPTER TWO

Crack.

The riding crop stuck Sir in the face. "Lazy slut! You stupid—"

"Sweet lemony koala pussy!" Sir screamed.

Crack. Mistress brought the crop back across his other cheek.

"Lana!" He pushed her out of bed, so she landed on the floor.

She scurried to the opposite wall of the room in fear. "What the hell's gotten into you?"

"You didn't observe the safe words!"

She ran milk-coloured fingers through her fiery hair. "What's the big deal, *Barry*?"

"Sorry, Mistress. Didn't mean to use your real name." He wiped the sweat from his brow. "The safe words are the hallmark of our trust. The reason I know that no matter how much you abuse me, I can stop it at any time. That I am, as much as you, the one who brings the abuse on myself."

"Well, if it's so bloody important to you. Hey, I know what'll cheer you up! Why don't you pick out today's activities?"

"I think *I* can assist with that!" boomed a voice from their window.

The pair turned.

A hippo in a smoking jacket appeared through the window, standing on hind legs upon a flying saucer. "Allow me to introduce myself. I am His Excellency, Hippo for Life, Real MC, Number One VIP, Lord of All the Beasts of Ecofallopialand and Giants of the Arid Venusian Surface and Conqueror of the Solar System in General and Venus in Particular, Boris Hippoman. But you can call me Boris."

"Such an honour." Mistress curtseyed as far as her night-corset and PVC shorts would allow. She took Sir's choke chain from the floor and lassoed it around his neck, tugging him to his swollen knees.

"Oh no, dear madam," Boris said, "it is I who have the honour. I witnessed your commitment to the prevention of fraternizing between species at our Australian arena yesterday. It is a prime concern of my brethren, to whom it would be my pleasure to introduce you post-haste. I wished to thank you personally."

Mistress bowed. "Oh yes! I am so thankful to own a slave as insatiable as Sir, but his horniness homes to the wrong signals sometimes."

"Wonderfully put."

"H-How did you see us?" Sir said.

"There are cameras in everything, old sport." Boris gestured with his glass of champagne.

The couple drew closer and observed, in its most magnified bubbles, little cameras.

Withdrawing a red button from a jacket pocket, Boris pressed it, and they watched out their window.

Outside were colourful, winding pastel paths; robotic canopies; printed mountains and their automatically pumped waterfalls; the hovering monorail and its capsule-shaped carts; and streams of happy zookeepers on Segways.

A deafening buzz indicated that it was default mode time.

The zookeepers' skins split open, the capsules collapsed, and the mountains and paths revealed camera shutter-like openings. Out came four-legged turrets of some deep blue metal. They were spider-like objects with four crude and sharp legs. They looked up towards Boris and assembled in army formation in the crescent-shaped main street of Tigon-Ligerville, a highly decorative prison for hybrid animals.

Sir and Mistress watched in awe. Drowsy ligers and tigons in their bathrobes poked irritated heads out the front doors of their semi-detached houses. They slammed their doors shut again in fear when they saw the robots.

Boris looked to Sir and Mistress. "I'd like to cordially invite you both to a charity event in my chateau. It's an all-day affair, and I couldn't help but overhear your uncertainty about the entertainments that today would bring."

"Your chateau?" Sir said. "Isn't that all the way by The Cat's Eye Nebula?"

Boris barked dismissively. "Nothing but a rumour I spread so I could keep my privacy. Eyes?" he called to the skies. "Fingers in ears, if you wouldn't mind," he said to the couple, who obliged.

A fleet of screaming eyes popped out the ground like violently expelled seeds, roaming around and spreading their somniferous song across the land. Patrons dropped like dominoes. Once completed, Sir and Mistress were the only two visitors awake.

Boris pressed his red button again.

The Cemetery for Every Extinct Animal—a mile-wide curved bowl of land in the park's centre—rose. The entire ground swelled from concave to convex as graves thrust into the sky. The very centre of this newly created hill ruptured, releasing a hovering chateau drenched in the purple goop of the alien cesspool beneath.

"Hop on, my friends." Boris' silver saucer expanded like a Jupe table to a larger area. It easily accommodated Mistress and Sir as they climbed out their window upon it.

Sir's bare shoulder touched against Boris, and he shivered.

The hippo's warm breath huffed out in surprise. "What's the matter, man?"

Sir turned to Mistress. "C-Can we see one last exhibit first?"

Mistress' eyes widened. She had no desire to appear impetuous before the great Hippoman. "Quickly, then!"

Boris took them to the zone of human-impersonating animals and animal-impersonating humans, the last of the zoo's offerings. The three of them toured the penguin and penguin fetishist exhibit. Real penguins waddled and did their thing, looking all crabby with those yellow, straw-like frowny brows.

Sir tried to grab Mistress's attention and tell her of his reservations when Boris wasn't looking—but it was no good. She was too engrossed by the humans waddling amongst the penguins. They wore jockstraps with orange pen caps taped to their faces in an approximation of a beak, coated in black and white body paint and licking droppings off plastic rocks. Some, high from snorting powdered flightless birdshit, dove from the rocks into the gangrenous sea of hungry, mutated megaseals below——prompting the joke:

Q: "What's black, white and red all over?"

A: "I'm offended."

Boris' patience wore visibly thin. His face rushed with blood, turning pink.

Mistress asked Sir, "Is that it?" But it wasn't a question.

He slumped his head and led the way back to the saucer.

Together the three sped towards the chateau over the fields, jungles, deserts and tundras of unconscious gimps.

Adventuroso, O. (3944). □*Is Venus Happy to See You?* Earth: The Journal of Pointless Astrophysics, pp1045-1046.

A whole bunch of sandwiched-in parallel universes caused Venus to appear extruded into a sausage shape that curved slightly—some reported "pleasantly"—upwards. Infinitesimal circumferences of the planet piled on top of one another, separating the planet's hemispheres.

When the finding was announced, the astrophysicists who discovered it talked about what an exciting and unprecedented development it was. They extolled its significance to their field and what we know about this universe and others.

"Can we interact with the other universes?" someone asked at the first press conference.

"Absolutely!" said a kindly elderly gent in the scientific crew. "We have an interface with the molecule-thick universe directly beneath us."

"So we can't like go to the alien's house or whatever?" said another.

"No, but we will be able to collect some fascinating data."

"About what?"

"We don't even know yet!"

Once people had been to their local Starbucks and collected their latest favourite beverage, without a sliver of interruption from any of the other universes, they decided that being really clever meant making mostly wrong hypotheses and getting super excited about stuff about which other people—despite their best intentions—couldn't give a shit.

CHAPTER THREE

"Welcome one, welcome all!" Boris said as he, Sir and Mistress approached the chateau, a gunge-coated jelly mould of a thing.

The ground jetted pearlescent purple space goop. This removed the chateau, the source of the very ground's infection, ensuring that the swelling would decrease. Sure enough, the land became concave again at a vertigo-inducing pace.

The goop turned rubbery and peeled off.

The intricate architecture of the chateau put Dante's Mountain of Purgatory to shame. Layers of buttresses and pointed arches ran between the ornate stained glasses of their corresponding clerestories. The images depicted an apparent battle between every animal imaginable and an even greater fleet of crossbred animal types.

The total number of possible initial animal crossbreeds was about 1,000,000 multiplied by 999,999. This represented all possible combinations of a million different types of animals. You select each of the million first guys and make them fuck a lady version of the 999,999 others left. Further levels of crossbreed are then accessible by making the products of all those initial fucks fuck each other and onwards until, according to a disgraced minority of scientists, a singular beast is created that experiences nothing but pain and ridicule. This was the "slippery slope of hybridization that leads to singular being of pure pain" hypothesis. It was the most common argument used in purebred supremacy propaganda. And the prime concern of Boris and his foundation.

The stained glasses depicted only about one percent of the possible initial combinations. Sir and Mistress didn't know this, and so were duly impressed by Boris' assertion that they were looking at the full set of potential mongrels being defeated by a battalion of purebred animals.

The pair followed each layer up with their eyes. The tip of the chateau wasn't visible at this angle. Instead, they were left looking at the wobbly portal that forever floated above Venus. It was big enough to envelop the planet at the slightest disturbance. The most prevalent theory was that it changed colour with someone's mood, but nobody knew whose. Whoever they were, today they felt the colour of autumnal sunlight on the browning leaves of shedding sycamores.

Upon entering the chateau, Boris observed Sir proudly as he paused to admire the cock of an epic tarantula hawk. It was a black, chitinous and thorny rhino horn-like thing mounted on a frame of dried cat jam.

The walls of the grand foyer were the teal of a cow's vomit after he regurgitates poisoned cud from Stomach Four all the way back and out his mouth.

A dusty old moose ass in a gold frame caught Mistress' attention. It farted perfume at regular intervals. She pushed her hair to one side to catch a fart spritz and giggled.

"Onwards!" Boris commanded, waddling them up his jagged staircase.

Sir tiptoed along, stifling yelps of pain.

"It's the finest tiger tongue. The heavily keratinized filiform papillae—or 'spines', if you will—that cause your feet so much evident trouble? Well, they serve an essential purpose here. I hope you'll stay to discover what it is."

Up the stairs, several doorways presented themselves. The mouthparts of living, gargantuan tarantulas served as curtains. The spiders' many glassy eyes above looked down on the couple.

At the clap of Boris' slimy forefeet, the mouthparts, like stubbier limbs of those same spiders, separated. The fangs extracted themselves from the floor, scraping along it and out the way so that Boris and the couple appeared to walk into a spider's jaws. But instead of spider guts, a tunnel lay beyond, which flowed the protective red of a womb. At the end of the tunnel was a big elephant cunt, teeming with large mites, ghostly white and transparent critters that skittered along the dry and pleated pachyderm lips.

Sir looked around in awe. "How did you ever get this thing through Venusian border control?"

"Oh, my people are *everywhere*, my boy," Boris replied.

He led them to a large dining room, where framed daguerreotypes indicated the respective animals' places at the large table there. A bear, a giraffe, a bison, a zebra and a fleet of thirty or so animals entered the room from shadowy entranceways. They found their portraits at the table and sat down.

To Sir and Mistress' surprise, Boris had daguerreotypes for them, too. Someone had zoomed in on each of them from a security camera's footage and printed their images on silvered plates. There was even a trace of a time stamp in the lower corner of Sir's.

Deers in maid's uniforms came in with enormous platters of living Troll doll soufflé, Furby fromage and the spinal columns of mice, specially treated with chemicals to make them edible. Sir dared not try any of the food, nor make conversation. He stared instead at the painted cyclorama that circled the dining table, its focal point a heroic and musclebound Boris, leading the pedigrees into battle against mongrels and hybrids alike. Sir found its experience humbling: the painter had clearly pored over it for years. Catching onto Boris' methods, Sir saw that Boris' depiction in the painting, which was more like that of a human male with a hippo's head, was probably a result of Boris not allowing the painter to see him naked, lest he got any ideas. But this made Boris look like the most hybridized of the bunch.

A whale skeleton hanging above them sang show tunes.

"Let me ask you, Sir," Boris said, "your penis—is it bifurcated?"

"Bifur—what?"

"Does it have two heads, boy?"

"I wish!" Sir looked at Mistress with excitement. He rarely found topics of interest between himself and her friends.

She pouted back at him, implying Boris was not going with this where Sir expected.

"I thought of doing some mods. Mistress gets bored with its appearance. Lemme show you what I got and I'll tell you what I had in mind."

He leapt onto his seat and whipped out his junk.

The entire table laughed.

Sir cowered. Sure, he probably had the smallest member of all these animals, but for a human it wasn't bad at all.

Boris dabbed his lips with a cloth napkin. "Yes, I bet you would like to do some modifications. I would recommend two heads, for then you would be able to penetrate both the vaginas of your beloved Koalita."

"Her name is Koalita?"

Boris picked up his china plate and dumped the pink Furby upon it in a nearby bowl of cat-piss punch. He flung the plate at Sir's head.

Mistress stood up and placed her hands gently on Sir's shoulders. She scolded Boris: "Hey! I'm the only one who can abuse him." She guided Sir back to his seat.

Boris' forefeet slammed on the table. "Koa-li-ta! That's the name of the one with whom you seek to fraternize! To make more mongrel beasts fit only to serve us this evening and for nothing else!"

Sir looked to the maids. They had not deer but human legs in those black tights. Human feet filled out their patent leather high heels.

"Sick satyrs," Boris continued. "Pitiless centaurs! Each half of them is an abomination which, fused with its abominated other half, creates a sin ever greater than the sum of its parts! Such is the synergy of evil of those miscegenators, masturbators and losers-of-life all!" Boris pressed his forefeet together, returning to his seat a little less heated, hippo cheeks draining of their flush. "My dear boy, we are not as savagely inclined as you. We find no other animals attractive but those of our own species. So, in a way I sympathize with your predicament. It's so easy for me to avoid fraternization, since I have no desire to partake. But you have a tougher battle on *your* hands."

A spectral silence of discomfort washed over the table.

"I quite fancy humans," a Bison said, her pelt spray-painted pink. "Little ones all dressed up in their formal gimp blues for a buffet?"

She batted her eyelids and Sir felt a wind roll off them.

"Oh-ho-ho!" Boris said. "You'll have to watch this one! She's feisty. I'm only kidding, Mistress. You'll see later this evening what we do to convicted crossbreeders."

"I-I kinda like squirrels?" said a timid, tuxed giraffe, scraping a knife through the dingleberry sauce left on his plate.

Another silence.

"I mean I would never act upon it, obviously." It was tough for giraffes to lower their heads in shame: they were so much higher than everyone else. "They're cute."

Sir squared his shoulders. "If I may ask, don't you think Gimp Week encourages the kind of behaviour you abhor?"

"Quite the contrary!" Boris said. "I think it's a harmless form of play that seeks to acknowledge the natural urge of humans towards bestiality and to discharge those urges in a healthy manner. And you know, humans are not the only ones partial to playfulness!"

"Are you ready?" a mongoose said.

"I think that's our cue!" said a fennec.

And so, for the animals, the fun began.

Hippoman, B. (3946). □*Staying Away From The Great Leader*. Venus: Ecofallopialand Press.

The following was mandatory reading for Ecofallopialand staff in the years preceding their complete automation.

His Excellency Boris Hippoman's nobility is as old as the singularity itself.

He came into this universe five hundred years ago, growing up in a utopian zoo on Planet Boris, out by the Cat's Eye nebula. The planet's surface is gilded. It rains diamonds, and pools of melted gummy bears are plentiful.

The sky turned pink in celebration and a platinum warship trailed a rainbow across the entire solar system. His Excellency stood upright on His hind legs and delighted his parents by speaking to them, informing them of his grand plans to improve the world into which they had brought him

At zero years old, there was no rush. So, He spent many years indulging in an idyllic childhood and concerning himself with small-scale tasks. He wrote fifty operas, directed a hundred of Hollywood's greatest actions movies and painted the biggest murals ever created. Awards quickly filled the seventeen mansions inherited from His parents.

He then invented burritos, Bombay Sapphire gin and the internet. Unfortunately, His followers became addicted to these great products. With dismay, His Excellency banned them, requiring citizens to volunteer any of their supplies to him directly. He would then have them executed. For their own good.

Using His divine powers, he created hospitals, fire stations and other amenities for His citizens. He made works of art so powerful that they reconfigured the synapses of evil men. He assembled an army of purebred animals which discovered and conquered new planets, cleansing them of inferior species.

Suitably pleased with these pursuits, it was time to begin His grand plan of intergalactic liberation by age eight. He started with the solar system.

First was Mercury. He purged the Caloris Basin of its macroscopic bacteria and melted its surface with his hot breath. He then bit into a rocky outcrop and sucked out the planet's molten core, shrivelling Mercury to an ultradense golf ball, which He took to Venus.

On Venus, He befriended the lava giants. He lit a peace pipe with their embers and exhaled across the planet's crust, a purple golfing green flourishing in the curling eddies of smoke. He then challenged the giants for ownership of Venus. With the peace pipe as His club, He struck Mercury with force and aim so true that He ultimately scored eighteen holes in one. After a first-attempt triumph like that, He never played the game ever again. Hence, he turned his attention to the construction of this great zoo, Ecofallopialand.

Unfortunately, His plan for total solar domination ended after the evacuation of Earth, a world of pure Evil. This purge was a monumental task even for His Excellency. When He learned of the debauched acts that took place there, between man and beast, He plucked a dandelion seed head from the ground and confessed to it every good deed of His life. The seeds, thus embittered by pure envy, flew to Earth and spread their sorrow across its nations. As its great scientists have documented, the seas dried up after this day, the parched earth cracked and the air condensed with suffocating humidity, cleansing the land of its infidels.

With the liberation of these three planets, as legends tell it, beings from the solar system's remaining habitats deduced their only options. They could flee in fear or congregate and worship. Thus, Venus became enriched by the greatest citizens the solar system had to offer.

Ecofallopialand was the natural home for these wondrous creatures, and Boris had no need to spread his influence further.

Venus' lowly koalas, in awe of His Excellency's brilliance, grovelled before Him. They knew themselves to be paupers but begged to stay in His presence. Magnanimously, He allowed them to remain as display pieces so that visiting royalty could remember their primitive origins and do everything in their power to avoid such a terrible fate.

CHAPTER FOUR

As Sir and Mistress suspected, the animals' brand of fun was the weirdly antiquated type from Victorian England. The chateau had reeked of this bullshit the whole time.

The games of charades, Pictionary and Who am I? had become obsolete millennia ago after interplanetary players attempted to wrestle with a Milky Way's worth of unwieldy history and culture. People had no references in common anymore. A single animal's life wasn't long enough to make but one connection with another in most instances. Life was too big.

Partygoers looked for something simplistic. Playing cards made a fierce return to the scene—Boris' favourite was Concentration, the pairing game. Mistress opted out, but offered Boris her whip to use on those animals who failed to locate a suitable pair. She later guided Sir away from the table when she saw that he was losing on purpose to get his ass torn up.

Once this phase of the party was over, the animals ran downstairs to a ballroom, where a fleet of at least a hundred more joined them.

Boris stood on the stage overlooking the room to explain a dancing game. Animals would head around the room in a circle and pass between partners beneath a special light that would scatter across them from a collection of spotlights on the ceiling. When the lights turned off again, Boris eliminated those who were not with their own species.

Sir wondered what the fuss was about the light. When they switched it on, he understood.

The room turned to a weird monochrome. A fleet of overlapping skeletons of various shapes and sizes faced him. The big prognathous jaws of gorillas. The strange, rat-like buck teeth protruding from elongated skulls. The elegantly ovoid eye sockets of gazelles that housed eyeballs floating like gelatinous ghosts beneath the room's X-ray light.

The dance began. Sir faced Mistress' glowing skull. She cackled and spun him around, throwing him off in the direction of what he figured was a bear. He clutched onto its claws daintily, nuzzling into its coarse, scratchy fur. It flung him with brute strength.

Now he was in the arms of a giraffe, whose forelegs held him limply. He sensed in the way the giraffe carried himself that it was the same who'd dared to reveal his delectation for squirrels at dinner. He looked up and nodded respectfully at its intimidating neck.

Off to the next. A draught told him he was near an open window. As he spun around, a figure with binoculars appeared there.

Four little fingers. Skull the size of two fists. The way it clung onto the window frame as if it was a tree branch. It was a koala!

He gasped and spun around again. His companion this time was surely a lion, and an overly friendly one at that. It pressed him into its mane as they danced. Sir squinted to keep the fur out of his face, but opened his eyes to look through the lion at the koala.

Its little marsupial claw pointed to the floor.

Sir clung to the lion and looked down. Several floors beneath, he saw human skeletons lined up like sardines, holding their wrists together over their pubic bones. It could've been the motion of the dance, but the bodies to which those skeletons belonged appeared to writhe. Sir looked back to the window, but the koala had fled. He had to find Mistress and escape!

"Okay, everyone! We're about to turn the X-ray off, so go find your partners!"

Sir ducked an embarrassment of pandas, a plague of rats and shielded himself against an unkindness of ravens. He barreled towards Mistress, seeing the outline of her slim hips through the skeleton of a—

The X-ray turned off and the regular lighting came on again.

Before Sir stood Boris, in a regal red ringmaster's jacket. "I should've counted on you to get it wrong." He held a metal hoop in his forefoot, which he slung around Sir's neck, dragging him off the dancefloor through a dense collection of ridiculing animals.

Sir landed on a stool. An elephant bartender offered him the chateau's speciality cocktail, but Sir declined.

Boris addressed the remaining pairs on the dancefloor. "Well done, everyone! What a raucous knees-up!"

Sir's new giraffe buddy and several other meek animals had joined him by the bar towards the end of the tenth round. Still no sign of Mistress. If they'd eliminated him, why not her?

"Here's to our guest of honour!" Boris ascended the stage, holding Mistress' hand in his. "I let her play on for that reason, naturally. Thanks to all of you for being good sports toward her this evening. Now we move onto the next phase, a favourite of so many!"

On the stage, tiger pelt curtains peeled back to reveal four chain gangs—two on either side—of naked humans. Fraternizers, without a doubt.

The chain gangs sang the famous music hall song "The Boy I Love is Up in the Gallery", substituting the word "boy" for animal names called out by the audience. Once disqualified for singing the wrong lyrics, Boris handed them a shard of mirror with which to disembowel themselves.

The first to do so was a young man in the leftmost gang. Boris flung out his forefoot and a shard of glass shot out his sleeve, slicing the man in the face. The audience whooped and cheered as he knelt to retrieve the glass and stabbed it into his abdomen. The chains around his wrists gently jingled, his hands and stomach bleeding as he carved himself a second mouth, guts flopping out for a tongue. Sir shuddered at its crimson lips.

The game progressed and more losers bled out. They dragged their chain gang members down by the stocks that held all their heads in a row.

Boris waddled along and strung their intestines around the other fraternizers like scarves or flung organs at the crowd who squealed in mock outrage at the act, licking the flecks of blood that hit their faces.

The music stopped and Boris whispered something to Mistress.

She took his mic and stood centre stage. "We have our winners!"

Boris released the last man and woman from their stocks and held up their hands. Their skins drained of blood, eyes filled with the panic of fight or flight—yet neither option was available.

"And now, the climax of the evening."

The animals tittered and watched fervidly as the surviving pair copulated for the audience's entertainment.

Mistress smiled like a magician's assistant as she held the microphone to the bloody, entrail-encrusted woman on top so everyone could hear her whimpers and sobs.

"Do they even know how?" murmured an ox to his wife, commenting on the female's underwhelmed insertion of the male's sexual organ.

The human male's head bucked back in agony.

"You'd think he could even pretend to enjoy it," the ox-wife said.

"See this?" Boris' eyes burned with crescents of low red light like a dying bonfire. "This is what it's all about! We're giving this beautiful couple here an EDUCAYSHUN! And so the male made himself fuck unto the female, and they were both the same species. And it was GREAT! Wasn't it?!"

Hippo spittle coated the man's body as Boris shook him into confessing: "I wish she was a sheep!"

The audience gasped. A murmur danced from one to the next like the passing of an electrical impulse.

"You know what that means, everyone!"

The animals squealed and ascended the stage to collect both bodies, running out the room and back through to the foyer.

Sir followed, in pursuit of his Mistress, to make sure she didn't involve herself—then he saw something abominable.

A pig, camel and cow gripped the male fraternizer. An okapi, two macaques, a warthog and an aardvark grappled their limbs around the female fraternizer. These animals stood as two teams at one end of an expanse of Boris' tongue-coated floor, facing the grain of those rough, spiny papillae. As the animals placed their bodies down, the man and woman screamed as the carpet's spines slid easily through their skin, bending like some natural Velcro.

Boris stood between both teams and held his forefeet up. Dropping them, he shouted, "Go!"

Both teams pushed their body along the floor. The room filled with the gritty sound of sandpaper against tooth enamel.

As both teams reached the end, the man's team had pulped the entire surface of the skin, opting for a rolling technique. This left a streak of blood of increasing width along their path. The woman's team focused only on one side of her, eroding half her exterior meat, scraps of leg muscle and breast fat caught on sporadic sprouting fibres. The teams raced back to the starting line and performed another stroke. The woman, now licked clean of all her skin, kept only some unsnagged internal organs. After this second pass, the man, so cleanly and evenly excoriated, still had all his muscles visible and untouched, as if some cruel machine exacted this punishment.

Boris' voice echoed across the foyer. "This was a competition to erode the flesh."

Tarantula mouthparts wriggled with pleasure.

"Both teams gave a great performance and got the job done in a record two strokes!"

A smattering of animal applause followed. Hooves, webs and paws made a sound both organic and surreal.

"As adjudicator, I favour craftsmanship. Stefan's team, for having so meticulously skinned the male, is the clear winner!"

Animals rushed in around both teams.

An orgiastic, champagne-swilling bloodbath followed. Hyenas tore at the remaining flesh. Vultures flocked in and picked at scraps. Lions gorged on livers. Elephants vacuumed up blood and gore.

"The throat of my mansion will clear itself," Boris said to Sir.

Pipes, poking out the wallpaper, spilt synthetic saliva into the tongue-floored room. Columns running around the room split in the centre, like two rows of teeth.

"Won't you come with me, son?" Boris added.

Sir didn't think hippos could wink, but those stubby little ears seemed to wag as Boris lit an apparently post-coital cigar and held out a free foot for Sir to hold.

Sir turned and grabbed Mistress' hand tightly. He could just run for the door.

Mistress reached out her free hand to Boris. "Aren't you gonna invite your guest of honour too?"

"Why yes, of course." Boris ushered them towards a door of varnished walnut.

Boris gestured for his human companions to sit on a dark green leather couch while he sat in an armchair. He lit the candles that lined his small writing desk, but kept the wet voids of his eyes on Sir. "I couldn't help but notice that you work out."

"That's thanks to Mistress. She doesn't like the way I look when I haven't done my nightly exercises."

"She's asleep when you do this?" He pulled out a half-empty bottle of bourbon and poured himself an enormous glass. A slight stagger hinted that he'd hit the sauce hard already. "Why, that *is* cruel! What a slavedriver you are, Mistress!"

He reached out with his cigar as if to sting her. She snarled.

Sir placed a hand on Mistress' leg, which twitched with discomfort. "Mistress, I haven't told you this"—he looked earnestly to Boris—"but sometimes I avoid exercise on purpose. So she has to whip me."

"Really, now?" Boris undid the sash of his smoking jacket.

She looked to the floor. "W-We do it for fun."

Boris' head rolled in a lazy circle as he spoke. "Yes, well, as you can see, we all have our curious notions of what *fun* entails. Now, I wonder, how exactly did you establish yours?"

Sir looked to Mistress for permission to tell their story. She nodded, so he began.

Note from Ecofallopialand Staff

ANYONE WHO SO MUCH AS BATS A SULTRY EYE AT ANY OF OUR KOALAS WILL GET TOSSED OUT ON HIS DISGUSTING ASS!

CHAPTER FIVE

To kids like Lana and Barry, childhood was simply something to bear until they could become who they were born to be. Wonders that they were, their hyperborean appetites for pleasure and debauchery came with no nature or nurture-based explanation.

As teens at the same high school—he a scrawny, malnourished shrew of a kid; she a fire-haired seductress in sequined ballet pumps—they mentally fornicated the first time their eyes met. Thereafter, they tossed schoolwork out of their brains with the same ease that they psychically tossed one another off in the hallways. She was a real-live sexy schoolgirl. He was one of the few kids switched on early enough for this fantasy to be a reality for the brief window when it wasn't creepy. But "non-creepy" wasn't the bag of these kids—so *he* became the sexy schoolgirl, she assuming his strapping nature with a strap-on.

They sat in each other's bedrooms after hours, planning how to get caught mid-bugger by their families, scheduling the arrival and departure of their parents and siblings day after day. With Mozartesque timing, they fervently awaited their doors bursting open for one and all to see her ball-deep inside him. He racticed holding her school dress across his non-existent breasts coquettishly in faux surprise at the sight of his brother, her sister, his mother, her father.

They felt something like creative exhaustion after getting caught in the act by every conceivable family member combo and took a long break from one another.

Years later, their relationship came to fruition. After a stultifyingly normal decade-long gap, they met again in the Anal Anthrax club.

It was a semi-secret leather bar, one of the middle-tier ones. About as classy a place as they could afford to attend, since they were simple receptionists by day–he for a cornershop that made lampshades from human skin, she for a VR videogame company that let customers go grocery shopping, but as celebrities.

The club had only one sauna, and the drug dispensaries were always out of uppers—though the quota of clean needles could never dip by law.

The Platinum Lechery area's red leather room was muggy with anonymous lovemaking. Barry and Lana both paid a pricey sum to exist there each year—but they got their money's worth, becoming fully embroiled in the club's scheduled copulations. They recognized one another's appendages through billowing sex-vapours.

Lana turned, with her cherry-red bob, to see Barry in full gimp suit strapped to the wall. Sexually charged stag beetles used their mandibles to poke, prod and please him in configurations both natural and un-.

Lana made the acquaintance of the rare-spotted dildo-tailed leopards of Mango Hills. They had their way with her as much as she did them. They were a veritably bestial *Cirque du Soleil* of sexual depravity.

It was the relative paradoxical innocence of the grins then-Lana and then-Barry exchanged across the room that bound them spiritually to one another thereafter. No matter the architecturocarnal masterpieces they and their anonymous partners built that evening, they never lost sight of one another. In fact, they directed their efforts towards each other, like male dogs fucking their rivals to demonstrate copulative prowess.

In the morning, all the walls flipped. The treadmill-type floor renewed itself for cleaning. The front doors opened, and the club exhaled all the evening's entropy like a greenhouse gas—but instead of degrading the ozone later, their sexual ether took aim at the nuclear family.

Leaving into the light, hand in hand, Barry and Lana earned their titles of Sir and Mistress. They returned later that day, when the place was a café, in their equivalent of sick-and-twisted costume: he in chinos and a button-down, she in a plaid blouse and mom jeans.

They shared a milkshake in silence and fucked psychically as they had at school. They used the sexual medium of eye contact in full view of the city's mothers and their terror tots. There they stayed, awaiting the return of Unsavory Night, staring at one another. The day's clientele left. The nighttime staff got nervous, thought there was some mistake. They couldn't recognize this pair with whom they too had participated in all manner of jerkings and penetrations—yet the unsavoury hours returned, and the couple seemed intent on staying. So everything flipped back out.

Back came the red walls, the stained floor. At that moment, Lana and Barry returned to their true identities of Sir and Mistress, stripped off and went at it again with everyone harder than before. The idea that they had survived a day of crushing banality together and could therefore do this forever and ever reinvigorated them. With charged batteries, they engaged in an all-night fuckfest with, it transpired, the coworkers of their respective Terran offices.

Mistress offered Sir a "lapdance." The room groaned at this tameness until they saw that to this pair, "lapdance" was code for him eating her poop.

Once literally shitfaced, they danced to Chris DeBurgh's "Lady in Red", knowing they were in love and that the evening's fun—its needle play, fisting and felching—soon had them in their natural roles of master and servant for good. They wanted to play like this forever.

How dare such synergy turn sour?

Reality's grind provided humiliations truer than anything they could act out. These two—who once frequently explored their flagrant coprophagic tendencies and near inhuman pain tolerances at all hours—would periodically develop calluses of fear in each other's continued company. They became afraid to so much as ask one another to do the dishes, when once polite requests for champagne flutes full of piss were the norm.

Life was the ultimate dominatrix. There was no safe word for what she had to show them.

They kept cute little corgis and other more metaphorical 'pets', but lost them all.

His infertility and her barrenness weren't biological; the bad chemistry was in their combined miasma, which wafted death and mediocrity wherever. The hedonism of their past pained them for real. It was practice for adult life, whose punishments were for all "boys", bad or good.

Life was a chatter, chatter, chatter of negativity and failed aspirations and endless confusion and disappointment. An icy type of woe formed in their stomachs and refused to melt itself, to expel from their faces in the form of warm and comforting tears.

Why? Where did it come from? When would it end? *Would* it end?

They longed for an era when the cruellest events of their lives were those they planned and exacted upon one another. But adulthood was the real deviant, only offering aftercare in the afterlife, if at all.

They scheduled their sessions, maintained their quotas of cruelty. But the artifice of it eroded. The insults, spitting and whippings were not acted but exacted, performed for real. It was the time they were most real with one another and fulfilled the hopes of their growing resentment. The real 'sessions' began when they were in pyjamas, side by side in bed. They stopped speaking, picked romcoms to watch that they both hated, and hated one another for absorbing them without complaint.

Maybe a holiday would fix it. A trip to Ecofallopialand. But how could they get away from it all if they brought each other with them? If they brought *themselves* with them? If escape was the end goal, they yearned to carve their consciousness out of these disappointing lives and vacate this universe. Nothing within it—not even within themselves—offered any solace.

Extract from Ecofallopialand Kidz Koalaughalong Joke Book, pp456-457

29854.
Q: How can you tell if ~~an elephant~~ a koala's been in your fridge?
A: Footprints in the ~~butter!~~ eucalyptus!

29855.
- Doctor doctor! My husband thinks he's a koala!
- Pull yourself together.

29856.
Q: Why did the koala cross the road?
A: It is the task that he, as a koala, must perform forever, fully accepting his burden. A car may strike him whenever, and time, inexorably thrusting him towards his demise, ultimately renders his suffering meaningless. But we must imagine him as happy.

CHAPTER SIX

"Wow." Boris stubbed out his cigar at the end of Sir's minimized and sanitized how-they-met story. "Finding someone that shares your ideas is a—" he sighed. "It's a miracle, really." He leaned back in his chair as he examined Sir and Mistress. "I bind my crew to me with hoops of steel." He gestured with his now-empty bourbon glass. "I wish the same to you both. I'll show you to your rooms and bid you goodnight."

Sir's face was hot with the sensation of having been stared at intensely for several minutes. "W-We can make our way back to the hotel alone."

"Hotel? No no, I can't have my guests staying in a place like that."

Sir and Mistress got undressed in their new bedroom in the chateau. They carried themselves wearily. The night had most definitely wound to a stop.

Naked, Sir slumped against the window, looking out at an enclosure below. It was a tropical playground for orphaned animals of all sorts. Children foraged brown recluses from steel trees for their toxic lunchtime salads, plucked tarantulas from fake foliage to microwave and slice open, filling them with cheese, like baked potatoes. The luckiest, who bore the swelter of the hunt-space long enough to spot a huntsman, could freeze him and munch him raw, the slowed action of his lagging limbs indicating—to the delight of otters, foxes, cheetahs and humans alike—that he was still alive.

Mistress caressed his neck with an idle hand. She smiled as he turned to her. "Look at this, Barry." She opened the wardrobe in the corner, revealing a long rack of silk pyjamas shaped like different animals. She scanned the labels on the hangers until she found the pyjamas for humans and pulled them out.

"Y-You don't mind if I wear them?" Sir stood shaking. "I know we don't have my exercise equipment here, but I'll stay up all night and do callisthenics. I might not maintain the tone you like, but—"

"Why would I—Barry, I'm sorry I disobeyed our safe words. I was afraid of losing you. That's why I avoided the rules. I'm still learning how to keep you with me and let you flourish."

He turned, leaning his elbows against the window frame. "I *should* take issue with the idea of you "keeping me with you." But I get it. Perhaps our fear of losing one another is why we operate with a more formally restricted method of conducting our relationship. The power struggle remains static if I volunteer all power to you, and you exert it always. The brutality of it, the cruelty of how we treat one another is really one of cowardice's stranger expressions. Or something?"

"Why did we adopt this lifestyle?"

"It was fun!"

She buttoned up her pyjamas with her back to him, sitting on the bed. "Not for us."

Sir walked to the bed and tore the duvet open with his teeth. He made a dog-style ball of blanket for himself in the room's corner.

Mistress stamped her foot to get his attention. "That won't be necessary. Stand down."

"What do you mean?"

"You can sleep in bed with me tonight."

"But—it's against the rules! Not just the fun ones we made for ourselves but also the big, overall rules! Humans aren't even allowed to hug anymore. Aren't you scared of getting scabies?"

She leaned back on the bed. "I'd bear an itch of seven times seven years for you."

He nodded, put on his pyjamas and climbed in beside her.

So she'd been extra cruel because she was uncertain of his love. Did that rejection manifest in a love deprivation? Did it make his eyes stray from their bed to the seductive, inflamed lips of koalamydia?

He held her so close, her softly conditioned hair fluffing around his face. His body encompassed hers, much like a microscopic male blood fluke houses its female during constant copulation after successfully penetrating the web space of a villager's toes.

This act of trusting symbiosis allowed sleep to find them.

Anonymous. (3012).◻*Torturous Parlor Games for Girlimals and Boyimals*. Anthropotomes vol IV (5), pp1038-1039

<u>Hissing Hippo:</u>
1. Guests strap a fraternizer to a massage chair with wheels and roll it to the centre of the room.
2. While still alive, the hostess saws the fraternizer's abdomen open. She then crams as many juniper berries between the viscera as possible, due to physical space or fraternizer resistance.
3. She pads the area dry and pours in gin to fill the cavity to its brim.
4. She sets the gin alight with a taper.
5. Guests must brave the flaming gin and pluck out juniper berries, cramming them into their ungrateful gubs.
6. Amusement ensues.

<u>You Gotta Have Balls of Steel to Populate the Stories We Tell This Dark Eve:</u>
1. Five tables are required for this game. From left to right, the following are laid out upon them: paraphernalia recovered from the homes of fraternizers, papyrus, candles, bowls of water, bottles of gin.
2. In the dark of night, each guest takes an object of paraphernalia and invents a story about it without hesitating or repeating words. As they do, the hostess lights a candle.
3. The story ends when the rules are broken, or the candle goes out (rare.)
4. The storyteller wraps the object in a papyrus.

5. They hold the papyrus and observe their reflection in the water, renouncing the spirit of the fraternizer that allowed the story's telling.
6. The gin is for guests.

<u>Everyone Suffers Somehow Always:</u>
1. Many versions of this game are possible. All versions require a collection of fraternizing and/or non-fraternizing animals (contestants) placed in an observation room.
2. The hostess typically tasks contestants with finding the fraternizer within their group. She may use non-verbal "prompts" until contestants understand the rules. She may ask questions, perform rounds of elimination or offer no explanation and let the situation degrade to absolute savagery. Guests may participate or silently observe from behind one-way glass.
3. Whether one, all or any of the contestants really are fraternizers is also at the discretion of the hostess—but almost any combination results in hilarity.

CHAPTER SEVEN

The gibbous moon shone a beam into Sir's eyes. He rose to see the curtains drawn back, the window open.

"Wait a minute," he whispered. He checked to see that Mistress still slept. "Venus doesn't have any moons! That's a torch!"

The torch dimmed, revealing its owner, sitting in the window frame's corner. "Shh!" A little paw guarded its mouth.

"Identify yourself,"

"You can call me Georges Waumbut."

"You were at the ball."

"Indeed I was. We have a friend in common. She wants to meet you."

"She does?" Sir pressed a hand to his chest, which rippled his pyjamas.

"But of course. Don't you want to meet her?"

Sir looked to Mistress. She tossed around, looking for her big-spoon-in-crime.

"I don't know."

"I can't make you do anything. But I can tell you this. I risked my little koala ass coming here tonight to find you and deliver this message, and I won't do it again. It's now or never. You're not even koala curious?"

Sir walked wearily to the window. "Of course I am."

"Of course you are." Georges' ear tufts shivered with delight. He slid down the drainpipe by Sir's window.

Sir changed into leather chaps and a matching waistcoat—since damage to the pyjamas would give the night's game away—and followed Georges.

They landed amongst the razor-leafed bushes that grew around the chateau's perimeter.

Georges took a pair of heat-resistant gloves from his utility belt and donned them. He then removed a canister from the belt and rubbed it until it sprayed a load of some hot wax over the bushes. He cooled this spray with a fan so they could pass through the ensuing path of neutralized leaves, which brushed them without harm.

Georges scurried up the sloping path of the surrounding graveyard.

Sir followed reluctantly. "Where are you taking me? Australiaville is in the opposite direction."

Georges smirked. "We don't live there the whole time. I'm taking you to a pore."

"Ew." Sir touched his face. He couldn't so much as look at one of the park's pore maps without setting off his trypophobia. He felt hollow, as porous as a prison sponge.

They snuck through the graveyard and slinked over sleeping solar tiles. Their night-time snores were digital reverberations through the pair's bare feet.

They hung upside down from the monorail line and climbed up high in the air. From there, Georges accepted Sir's hand and dragged him atop one of the rail cars. At their height, the wind was refreshingly chilly, the ground beneath at a dizzying distance.

Georges took out his binoculars and scanned the ground. The world within the glass tree was big enough to have its own weather system. Thin clouds hovered over the graveyard's wasteland, casting their sorrowful shadows wide across the night's dead park.

"There!" Georges pointed to a small, black ellipse cordoned off by orange warning beacons.

"That's where we need to get to?"

"Now, follow me," Georges revealed his grey premolars in a wide grin. He held his arms above him and dove towards the pore. To Sir, he shrunk with distance to the size of a summer tomato as he disappeared into the pore's shadowy entrance.

"Shit!" Sir stretched his legs as if to trick his mind into preparation. He stood up, took a deep breath, and jumped.

Wind whistled around his ears. He turned to look up and cheered with awe.

The display of fake sky faded. He saw lava giants roaming the planet's surface through the tree's glass. They were more subdued than he expected. The clubs extending from their arms smoked lazily and the bulky rocks of their surface floated around, revealing cracks of their angry lava core.

A thick cloud meandered into Sir's path. As he burst through it, bullets of rain and the echoes of an epic storm consumed the environs. He could no longer see or direct himself towards the pore. The constant film of rainwater wouldn't clear from his face as he accelerated, at Venus' frightening pace, towards the unyielding ground.

DeGrasse TysonBot III, YaBoi, TheScienceGuy, Guccisubushi et al. (3254). *Extract from On Human Hazards.* Earth: Nature, pp-5356-5358.

<u>Origin (history and morphology):</u>

From as long ago as 1990 AD, koalas have been infected by the *Koalamydia trachomatis* bacterium. Transmittable through sexual contact, mother's milk or both, it can cause blindness, infertility and "wacky dance."

As is now common knowledge, due to unclear factors associated with their acclimatization to the planet Venus, koalas developed second mouths on the left sides of their abdomens. Or the right, if homosexual. These allowed the koalas to better adapt to Venus' conditions for obvious reasons. They also led to bizarre new mating rituals, facilitating mass exposure to koalamydia.

Indigenous Venusian koala populations are infected by koalamydia at rates of 100% or more. The second mouths' lips become red and inflamed in the infected, which allows for ease of diagnosis.

For what possible reason, you may ask, has the author chosen to squander his obvious talent writing about this?

The reader is advised not to dismiss this text. This paper outlines salient information on our most recent discovery: Koalamydia has crossed the species barrier and now poses a threat to humans. How this happened is a strange and harrowing tale.

Introduction:

The first human to display symptoms of koalamydia was a member of our original research group and a personal friend.

Ignatius Pheochromocytoma was a Terran scientist who came to Venus to study how koalas had acclimatized to their new planet. He was an English gent with a carefully teased black moustache, and he wore wire-rimmed spectacles.

Soon after arriving on Venus, he stopped leaving his camper van. He would no longer respond to us when we knocked on his door. Looking through the window, we saw him in stained underwear, whooping and throwing a ball of paper at a basketball hoop he had constructed from a pillowcase and Sellotape.

We saw something trailing from his underwear and assumed it was toilet paper—but once we broke into his van and tackled him, we discovered it was a satin ribbon about eight feet long. It took four teammates to fully restrain Pheochromocytoma and extract it.

We quizzed him as to the ribbon's origin. He fed us some excuse about a supposed experiment of his: chopping up a koala to see if they had souls. He gestured wildly as if to show them where he had nicked his hand with a cleaver. Indeed he had suffered some injuries. However, this lie about the mode of disease transference would be far more convincing if we hadn't found sautéed koala meat in his rectum. Not to say the chopping didn't transfer the disease, but Occam's razor dictates the likelier cause.

In doing so, he spoiled "everyone's fun." Nowadays, human-koala contact is explicitly forbidden.

Those cute-faced, dozy lil' bastards will fuck your life up.

CHAPTER EIGHT

Sir screamed. "Ahh!"

George pawed at his face. "Dude, relax. We made it. You landed safely. You slipped into the pore and we provided enough upthrust to counteract your velocity."

"Who did?"

Sir opened his eyes. He was in the blunt tip of a long cuboidal sandstone chamber, lit by camping lights at even intervals placed along the wall. The chamber curled off at the end, the rest of its path occluded by its curvature.

He sat up and examined his arms. A painful purple bruise streaked through his skin like marble. Looking at his hands, he saw a koala's paw reach out. He pushed it away, but a voice reassured him. "It's okay."

In front of him stood a koala in a Hawaiian shirt and no pants. Around the frames of its cheap wayfarers, with luminous yellow arms, were the dark shards of its smashed lenses that glinted with the same ferocity as the eyes.

Sir accepted his paw, and the koala helped him to his feet.

Georges leaned on the wall, nodded emphatically, giving non-opposable appendages up.

"My name is Dis Koalawannaleya."

Sir frowned. "Can you say that again?"

Georges hissed. You didn't ask Dis to repeat himself.

"I didn't expect a member of the speciesist humanarchy to pronounce my traditional koala name properly. But I bear no grudge. You are here and will be, for however limited a time, amongst us, learning. That's all I ask for. Come."

Sir followed Dis along the curving chamber. It led to a large inverted wedding cake-like structure, layers of staggered steps cutting deeper in the earth and drawing to some tip far beneath.

Shadowy square tunnels channeled off from the wall's base. Sir examined the symbols on the sandstone walls. Yes! They were inverted and reversed versions of Boris's stained-glass tableaux images.

Sir made this remark to Dis.

Dis nodded. "Indeed. We koalas live in the female mould that they used to create Boris' house of hatred and outdated tradition. To us, these inverted images of his stained glasses show a rain of hybrids falling upon Ecofallopialand's bourgeoisie. And this is our most fervent desire, for I am the ruler of this inverted kingdom. Here, we plan a koalavolution against those who seek to suppress the natural order of things, which is what?" He held a paw to his ear.

"Man lying with beast!" the koalas chanted, cheering Dis.

Dis laughed. He raised his hands in triumph.

Together, he and Sir walked the sloping path down each layer towards the koala hive's base. There, they sat on curved benches carved from felled redwoods. Sir placed his feet on the ground, feeling the warmth of its stony tiles, perhaps heated by some ingenious Roman-style network of hot water pipes.

"One of my colleagues noted that you, a human, indicated sympathy for our message of bestial love. When I heard that, I had to meet you."

Sir leaned forward. "Because I looked at a koala?"

Sir heard someone scoff. He turned to see Georges again. Dis demanded absolute respect. Opposing beliefs were unwelcome in his company.

"Hahaha!" Dis looked up at his followers, who peered over the ledges of each of their layers and laughed with him. "Your modesty amuses us, Mr Sir. This is no temple of properness and decorum. It is the very opposite of such a thing. The anti-chateau!" He placed his paws on his knees. "Be frank. It was more than a look."

"It was."

"Because of the absolute secrecy our koala militia requires, we would not have brought you here on a hunch, oh no." Dis moved to blow out the fire of a nearby pit and remove an ember-laden charcoal piece to draw on the ground. "This is Venus, no?" He drew a curved sausage, and then a wavy line above it. "And here is the portal above us. By our calculations, entering the portal will create a connection between our demi-universe and the one which contains *our* planet's lower half."

"Why would we want to do that?"

Dis placed a paw over his heart. "For that is the half of the universe where we left the acceptance of our kind. Before the rift cleft our planet in twain, we had a temple there where we would perform the most beauteous orgies. After the divide, we got stuck here, in this backwards hemisphere in which activities so sacred to us are forbidden. We must return."

"How?"

Dis sketched a star in the upper half of their Venus. "We koalas have used our expert knowledge of nuclear fusion to construct a plant at Venus' very core. When the time comes, we will make a thermal rocket of this planet and send it hurtling through the portal. Like a mouth in search of an ass ripe for eatin', as the saying goes." Dis' head drooped with dismay. "However, our safety tests are currently inconclusive. We require at least another week."

"I'm leaving in the morning."

"You can't! You must delay. Make an excuse. Do anything within your power to ensure you come with us!"

Sir exhaled sharply. "I-I don't know that you want me in your utopia. Really. Your secret's safe with me, but I should get back now. My girlfriend and I are in a good place and—"

She appeared. Just the glint of her shiny eyes in a doorway's darkness at first—but then her soft, chocolate fur came into view, as did her delicate paws and the lusciously inflamed, pouty lips of her second mouth.

Dis took off his sunglasses and shook his head about. "Need I say more?"

Koalita leaned on the frame. "Thanks to severe sexual droughts, my bush is on fire."

Entranced, Sir staggered towards her. She rubbed herself up and down the wall, the kink of her abdomen in this movement making her second mouth smack its lips. She beckoned him towards her with her paw. They disappeared into her bedroom.

He leaned down to speak with her—but he shut his mouth when he felt her soft paw brush his lips. Now was the time for actions, not words.

She lay down on a bed of torn-up truck tires.

He climbed on top of her, kissing her on the fluffy forehead and running his hands up and down her sides. His right hand stopped as he touched those red lips. They gave off heat to rival that of her genitals, which he could feel pressed against his bare stomach. Her belly's tongue lapped at his arm.

He caressed each of its enlarged human teeth, the mountainous peaks of the canines, the rough, undulating valleys of the incisors at the back. No gag reflex, he noted. Auspicious.

Rolling him onto his back, she mounted him and turned on her side.

"Ever get blown by a sidemouth?" Velvety air rushed past her honey-coated throat as she spoke.

He trembled with sexual thrill.

She lay on her mouthed side and rolled over him, the wet enveloping warmth of the mouth engulfing his throbbing dick.

He leaned back and closed his eyes, arms behind his head, thrusting into her. Oh God, Dis was right! Could pleasure like this become the purpose of his existence? He could never have imagined such a sweet fate until a koala sucked him off.

She stopped, clambered off him and pushed him up.

"What?"

She lay down on the tires and spread her legs, paws stretching her genitals open. "Eat my wet koala pussy."

Sir leaned over her and approached her mound. "Oh, my koala beloved. I'm gonna make you feel so good."

He pressed his lips to her cunt and let his tongue dart out, exploring the regions of her double vagina. She squealed like a bitten squeak toy, which got him heated.

He got up on his knees and towered over her, the flickering light of the lamps waving the shadow of his enormous prick over her.

She gasped, cowering at the potential of a human member compared to the stubby, split appendages of her own species, of which she had grown so tired. She rolled onto her back and got her legs in the air.

He approached, pushing the head of his dick inside her.

She panted, and he withdrew a little, allowing her koala tissues to deal with the shock of an immediate stretch. They looked into each other's eyes, panting, and she nodded. Once she overcame the girth of the thing, no amount of length bothered her.

He pushed himself into her, up to the base, turned on by her moans that got louder with each new inch of his that she experienced. He thrust.

"Split me in fuckin' two, you little human bitch!"

Nastier than he expected—and he liked it! Docile, eucalyptus-chewing koala-from-next-door by day; saucy little Koalita, the marsupial slut, by night.

He pounded in her until he was close.

She pushed on him with her paws to signal that he should remove himself. She then lay down on her front so he could mount her from behind.

His dick slipped into her second pussy, which had retained its tightness. It felt like fucking her open anew.

He lay down on his back. She climbed on top and alternated his thrusts between both of her inner chambers, diddling herself silly with one paw when she saw that he was excited almost to completion. As the inner walls of her cunt contracted in orgasm, he filled her tiny internal reservoirs with his cum until they distended and he could see her belly pulsing with each new shot inside her. When he was done, she bore down and cum flooded out of her and all over his dick.

"So you see now?" She panted.

"Holy shit. I've been doing it wrong this whole time."

"You know what they say! Once you go koala..." Her face fell when she realized it wasn't a real expression and had no end.

They sat in silence. Soon, he was crying.

"What is it?" She massaged him with her paws.

"When my girlfriend finds out about this—"

"The one that whipped you in the face?"

"She's promised she's gonna be sweeter to me in future."

"If you say so." She lay back on the bed. "I bet Boris has already beheaded her."

Sir gasped. "What?"

She shrugged. "You mean you hadn't figured it out? Didn't you see what he does to your kind?"

"But we never fraternized! I mean, I hadn't when I arrived. Why didn't you tell me it was unsafe?"

"Because then you would've left with *her*!" She cried with squeaky squeals like "Wheee!"

He stroked her head while she recovered.

"It's so unfair. Why couldn't I have met you when you were single?"

"I get your frustrations. But you should've told me all the same. I'm sick of being manipulated like this."

"You may find our aims extreme." Dis stood in the doorway, admiring the human specimen as if Sir was in the zoo.

Sir pulled his waistcoat over himself to hide his shame.

"But we are a reasonable species," Dis continued. "Now you know what we are offering, Georges will take you back to the chateau, and you can decide what to tell your girlfriend. We leave in three days." Dis smiled at Koalita. "I'm not the only one who would love to take you with us, Sir."

Sir nodded and got dressed. He kissed Koalita on the forehead, and Georges led him out.

Luckily for Sir, the route back to the chateau was much simpler—but it entailed the same level of bravery. Georges tamped some nuclear waste into a cannon with a lead sheet, which Sir stood on. Georges then set the trajectory for the cannon and retired to a safe space.

"Are you sure about this?" Sir shouted to him.

"Pretty sure!"

"Huh?!"

"We've never done this with a humaaa—"

Sir fired towards the Gothic chateau. It loomed large against the panorama of the encroaching, orange dawn. So early in the day and already the humidity rose, his velocity making a fierce wind of the otherwise still air. The slightest fleck of dust whipped across his body with frightening speed. He screamed through his nose to keep out the flies, closed his eyes and balled up as his bedroom window expanded before him.

He smacked against the bedroom ceiling and landed on the carpet.

Mistress woke up with a start.

"So sorry." He stripped from his clothes and flung them under the bed before she could register anything.

She rubbed her eyes and opened them to discover him with half a pyjama trouser leg on, wrestling with the other. "Get those off!"

"Huh?"

She tore the duvet in two, following the motion of his first bite, and tossed half in the corner.

"P-Please."

She mocked him "'Please' what? I saw how Boris looked at you last night. And, well, I know what sick shit you're into—I couldn't have it!"

"You just wanted to keep me! You have no interest in who I am. To you, I'm some—"

"Lapdog?" She took his leash out of the bedside table.

"We're going to talk about this in the morning."

"Only if it pleases me." She affixed an eye mask to her face and turned away.

He curled up on the scrap of duvet in the corner. Now that it was getting warmer, he could happily sleep until morning and decide what to do afterwards.

"What the Hell Happened?" An Ecofallopialand plaque on the history of Earth

1. The Human Soup Phase: Earth's polar ice caps melted

and the sea level rose. And rose and rose and rose. It swallowed the lands and created a liquid-surfaced planet with a roiling, boiling sea.

2. What Lurks Beneath Is Pissed Phase: The hole in

the ozone layer propagated across the entire atmosphere and depleted it. UV rays blasted the sea and evaporated it, drying up all the oceans. Giant squid, mega krakens and mammoth whales rolled onto shores like single-beast tsunamis, collapsing houses, forests and other critical infrastructural components.

3. Space Food Planet Phase: Every remaining molecule of

water evaporated from everything. All remaining creatures, who had failed to evacuate earlier, died. Their remains desiccated and floated in the breeze. The planet became a handy stopping station for free pick-me-up snacks for aliens on interplanetary trips.

4. Chill Out Phase: Stubborn humans returned and

attempted recolonization. They created isolated, safe hubs with breathable air and other essentials. One square foot of Earth is cultivated per annum. This makes ten in total to date.

CHAPTER NINE

Sir awoke to a growl and the sour smell of alcoholic hippo breath.

He looked above him and saw the hulking outline of Boris, who grabbed him by the foot and dragged him. Boris gripped the neck of a Bombay Sapphire bottle in his other paw, three quarters the way depleted.

"Mistress!" Sir screamed.

Her arm and leg dripped off the bed with a deeply unconscious slump. Boris had no doubt meddled with her.

Boris dropped Sir in an elevator.

"The fuck do you want with me?"

As they descended, bubbles of intoxication emerged from Boris' ears and floated around him. His smoking jacket was askew. His pants were off, large greasy hippo bollocks quivering with frustration. "You dare talk to me like that!" He held up a forefoot as if to strike Sir. "I know who goes where in this place. The pressure plates in your room told me you left for several hours. Now, for whatever reason, thousands of my cameras deactivated, from your window all the way to one of the monorail cars. And there are fingerprints on my windowsill, belonging to a koala or a human baby."

"A human baby."

"Why?"

"H-He was looking for his mother?"

"Then why are my bushes outside coated in koala jizz?"

Ting! They arrived in the basement at such a depth that Sir felt the pressure in his ears adjust. He fell back down to the floor as Boris yanked his ankle.

Boris dragged him across the rough, un-sanded floor of cement. It scraped his back with some discomfort. Luckily, Boris found his destination before the scrapes on Sir's back got deep enough to bleed.

Boris locked the door behind him, picked Sir up and strapped him into an execution chair.

Boris growled, taking a swig of gin. "Whooop." He flipped a switch and the room's halogen light burned Sir's eyes.

"What?!"

"Whoop! Whoop for me!"

"Whoop."

Boris slapped Sir's face with both forefeet. "No! Whoop! Whoop harder!"

"Whoop!"

"Gibbon-like or other? Inconclusive."

"What the hell are we doing here?"

"You know!" Boris walked behind him.

Sir heard the creak of a cabinet door, the removal of several clanging implements. His slimy paw came back and tugged down Sir's mouth as he inserted a sizeable plastic hose. At the hose's other end was a funnel, into which Boris poured some chemicals from a hazardous bottle.

"Mm!" Sir protested, but swallowed the chemicals.

When Boris yanked the hose out, Sir learned the purpose of the implement. His bowels vibrated with discomfort, on the cusp of evacuating themselves in emergency.

"Poop for me."

"Only Mistress can do this to me!"

"Oh, come on, she's never going to know! And what choice do you have? I'm only doing this to see if you poop a white ribbon. I'm testing you for koalamydia."

Boris tugged on Sir's thighs, his face inches from Sir's anus, which puckered.

Sir felt a ribbon emerging. It was somewhat absorbent, reluctant to leave as it adhered to the moist walls of his rectum.

Boris coaxed it out. "It's red."

WEIRD FAUNA OF THE MULTIVERSE

The inflammation caused by the searing tailpiece had damaged his linings so much that the ribbon absorbed blood on its descent. What luck!

"I'll have to make you shoot hoops, then. But first, let's not let this test go to waste." Boris took the tip of the ribbon in his mouth and drew suction on it like it was a strand of spaghetti, eating the nuggets of shit that soon followed. Not soap on a rope but shit on a ribbon. Delicious.

Sir squirmed in the chair. "You're a hypocrite! How is it that you care so much about whether I fucked a koala and yet here you are consuming my shit. In my world, that's much more intimate. Explain yourself!"

Boris moaned. He was in another world now, one in which even his own rules had ceased to exist. He channelled the strange, amnesiacal mental space a psychopath enters before a kill. "You fucking fraternizer!" His hippo lips were up against Sir's asshole now, lapping at it with his broad, hippo tongue. "Fraternize all over me, you sick, fraternizing fuck!"

Sir pulled away from Boris as far as his restrictions allowed. "I'm—not—hipposexual!"

Boris cried as he lapped away. "Oh, come on. If you were going to sleep with an animal, why not me? Do I repulse you so?"

Sir looked to the doorway behind them. Large safari ants crawled in and pooled just behind Boris.

"Yes. You disgust me."

Boris gasped and stumbled back, his black and empty eyes haunted. He stood in the pile of ants. They coated his lower limbs, shearing through his skin with their jaws, soon revealing the bloody bones of his legs and oddly elegant little trotter-like assimilation of foot bones.

The ants stripped Boris of his flesh all the way up to his belly, then formed two streams that burrowed inside him. His stomach bloated as they emerged again through his belly button, through the crook of his armpits, through his mouth. His eyeballs burst and splatted Sir with jelly, soon revealing the rest of his bones.

Boris made the strange glitchy sound of a talking teddy bear after accidentally going through a washing machine cycle. Soon, he had no respiratory system. The ants were now three, four times their initial size.

The ligaments and tendons that had held Boris' bones together now consumed, the bones themselves piled into an unceremonious pyramid in the corner.

The ants lumped together.

Sir protested, "No!" until they took on a familiar shape, the giraffe from dinner.

"Sir," the giraffe said.

"You came for me?"

"H-He always does this." The giraffe clacked his hooves together. "I never had the strength to do anything about it before." He took the restraints off Sir and went to the cupboard to find a medical smock, which he helped Sir put on. "But then I saw in your eyes the love for Koalita, how Boris wanted to put you down that night. I thought, 'Enough!' We all know what he's been up to in this basement of his. We all live in fear of him. We're all deferential and shit, and why? Fuck him, Sir! You go get yours, okay? Let's get out of here."

Sir hugged the giraffe, who gasped initially, the arbitrary rules of fraternization so ingrained in him.

"Lead the way," Sir said.

From "Snufflication for Beginners", an information post in The Cemetery for Every Extinct Animal

The following is a special mummification to commemorate the last corpse of a species. Cost and time are no object when it comes to mourning a new extinction.

1. Dander or feathers are collected from the body with a special wire brush. These are tightly wound into a bandage made from thinly sliced wood, which is then set alight.
2. The body is shaved or plucked entirely. The hair is washed away with gin. This stream pours through a small opening in the ceremonial room's floor, which is typically made from baked guano or similar.
3. The body is placed in a big bowl carved from sandstone.
4. Monks surround the body and throw stones at it until it is completely pulverized.
5. They pick up the bowl and carry it over to a coffin, pouring in the body and rocks.
6. The high priestess, usually the eldest female monk, dons her ceremonial gear: elaborate chains of thick rubies and

equivalently opulent jewels. She uses "deadie mix", a sacred powder of okapi ash and sea salt, to cover the body.
7. After five hundred years, monks return and

volunteer a "biggie token", a sacred childhood object—a mother's desiccated heart, favourite Game Boy Game or similar—placing it into the coffin.

8. The lid is lifted and secured using staple removers,

hammered into the wood. The box is thereafter referred to as a "snuffle container."

Only one final death will deviate from this process: that of Boris Hippoman. When He dies, the planet will become his tomb. One team of monks will unearth all the snuffle boxes and give them to space monks to put in their spaceships. Space monks will then assemble wooden planks around the planet and use snuffle containers glued to spikes to hammer the planks together, encasing the planet forever. For with His extinction comes the extinction of everything any one of us on this planet ever cared about.

CHAPTER TEN

They took the lift to the chateau's mouth. Sir marvelled at how completely the saliva cleansed it, no sign that anyone got gored the night before.

Shouts, bullet-fire, bombs, screams.

"What the hell is going on?" Sir said.

"The koalas," the giraffe said. "They knew you were in danger. You triggered the early koalavolution."

The giraffe smirked and beat his chest. He was a koala sympathizer.

Sir hadn't been taught the hand signal, so he just smiled politely and nodded.

They opened the chateau doors and walked out into the graveyard, overlooking the early morning's chaos.

Koalas tore a purgatory out the misty bowl of the morning's wasteland, swarming on park visitors en masse. Sir watched as a gimp in red leather ran screaming across the grass. A koala in a toga chewed on his ear, while another koala eviscerated the man with needle-like incisors.

"*Vive la révolution!*" screamed a koala as she flung razor-laden boomerangs at Boris' robotic fleet of drones.

"Koala power!" screamed another as it tore through a tank with its diamond-tipped claws.

In only some small hours, the koalas had incited human hatred amongst the other animals as well. Vultures displayed their flagrant disregard for the wellbeing of their imitators, the leather harness- and feather-clad humans. These humans flapped and ran, hoping to take off, only for their most beloved creatures to drag them to the ground.

Wasn't that how love ended up for most? Lovers discovered overnight the sudden and surprising inversion of love's nature.

Suddenly, every vulnerability freely expressed to their partner, which they'd thought was accumulating into a bank of trust, had swirled into an insidious hold of ammunition, then duly unloaded with wrath. The everyday human marriage dissolution appeared more civil, more cunningly calculated—but it was nothing more than what Sir witnessed now: the resentment, from decades of subjugation, expressed violently.

About ten horses each had groups of two men in front of them. The men wore pantomime horse costumes that bent over gravestones. Real horses buggered them to death, screaming, "This is what you wanted, isn't it?" Their enormous horse cocks ruptured the men's bowels with ferocity as they unloaded greasy, stinging horse spunk in the offending mortal wounds of their enemies.

Sir spun around three-sixty, observing bloodshed all around. Outside, the red dawn and the wandering lava giants, whose rocks had dissolved back into boiling magma, turned the scene into one of Boris' epic cycloramas. If ever there was one, this was a hideous, crystallized horror that merited oil-painting commemoration.

A fleet of flying squirrels in carpet bomb-formation flew across the sky, dropping plastic bags with piranhas in them. The bags glinted on descent like the diamond rains on Planet Boris.

"Let's go!" The giraffe scooped Sir up and put him on his back. Together they galloped against the graveyard's gradient, soon reaching its lip and entering the park proper.

Sir climbed up the giraffe's neck and stood on his head. They wandered the streets at a more casual pace. Sir stood with surprising stillness upon the giraffe's head. That was thanks to Mistress' training, how she used to make him stand atop a pole like a Buddhist monk in prayer. He revelled in the use of this training now, balancing upon one foot, one hand, laughing with glee.

The pastel streets presented an eerie calm. The occasional smears of already browning blood, of halved humans not seconds from death, were signs of a party already ended. Sir followed the dark tributaries to their source, the chateau's entrance where the atrocities had congregated like flies to shit.

Looking above him, Sir saw koalas tied to colourful collections of helium balloons all converging on a nearby hillside. "There!"

They galloped through the streets and up the hill to meet the koala militia.

After depositing Sir where he needed to be, the giraffe sped away, perhaps in the direction of his home, a family, he didn't say. He was gone before Sir could ask.

"Sir!" It was Koalita. She broke the formation that looked towards Dis, who delivered some type of sermon.

Sir ran and scooped her up in a hug. "What's happening?"

"It's glorious. We're going now, to re-join our other half."

"But I thought we weren't ready!"

"Worry not." She stroked his face. "I have faith that Dis will show us the way."

"I don't know."

"Brethren!" Dis adjusted his broken sunglasses. "Now is the time for our awakening!"

He took out a little device with a red button and pushed it. Behind him, the hillside opened and a bigger red button appeared. The koalas rushed in and pushed that one with all their strength. A mighty boom shook the ground beneath them.

Koalita grabbed onto Sir. "It's happening."

All the pores revealed themselves. Their nuclear light shot through the ground, beams of green firing out into the night sky.

"Lie down!" Dis commanded.

Sir dropped in a brace position, but Koalita encouraged him to flip over.

"Look up," she said.

Beyond the glass tree were the sun and stars, embedded in the blackness of space. The portal above shone with that same blinding, nuclear green. Their half of the planet gained thrust, pinning Sir and the koalas to the very ground, and they powered upwards. Soon, the portal was all they could see.

Dis shouted over the ensuing roar. "You'll want to close your eyes—but don't! Don't miss this!"

It was true. The portal was too bright, exponentially so as they approached.

The glass tree went into it first, its outline sparking. The portal engulfed them all, the ground, and all Lower Venus.

All the light snuffed out, and their world was pure darkness.

The thrust diminished, and they could stand again. The silence was so palpable that Sir was afraid to break it. He looked up and tugged his smock around him to stave off the encroaching chill of this new universe. Looking around, he saw only koalas with mouths agape in happy awe.

"Did it work?" Sir said.

Somewhere in the pack of koalas, he heard Georges smack himself in the face. Sir had questioned Dis' strategy.

Dis walked over to him. "Do you see it now?"

Ahead of them in the sky was a little blue scratch. It shimmered like a butterfly's wing as it caught the light. The coin of it expanded. It was Venus' other half.

"Phase two!" Dis shouted.

The koalas clambered towards an entranceway that appeared in the rock beside them. A mist streamed out from it, soon dissipating to reveal a silvery rocket lit only in the dim starlight of this new demi-universe. The land on which they stood was but a relic of some other era whose evil demagoguery had extinguished.

Hundreds of koalas rushed in a stream through the rock's opening. Sir ran with Koalita on his back. They laughed joyously, running up the industrial metal staircases, painted in warning colours. They filtered into the rocket, which pointed straight up in the sky.

They climbed up rungs embedded in the floor and into their seats. Sir sat at the back, separate from Koalita, since only a few seats could hold non-koala passengers. She scrambled further up the rocket to the front, blowing him a kiss before sitting down.

Dis took the controls, and Sir felt thrust again. It was nowhere near as powerful as the earlier blast. It felt as if he'd been driving on a motorway for an hour then got out of his car and ran as fast as he could, the incremental distance on foot relatively unimpressive. And so, a trip by rocket, an idea that had always terrified him, became tame in practice. He hoped his continued adventures would similarly cause his life thus far to pale in comparison.

"Forty-five minutes to landing," Dis said. "You may now unfasten your seatbelts."

Sir un-clicked himself from his seat and climbed up the aisle to find Koalita, eager to share every moment of this new experience—heck, eager to share *everything* with her!

Creeping up the rows of seats, he heard a familiar voice, and laughter. His heart dropped at the flick of her hand.

He sped up his scrambling, gripping onto her seat, scaring her. "Mistress! What the hell are you doing here?"

She looked at him, shocked, adjusting herself in her koala-sized seat. She and Koalita laughed.

Koalita flashed Sir a congenial smile. "It's fine."

"We talked things over." Mistress waved a dismissive hand. "It was selfish of me not to see that you are more than I can provide. You need Koalita in your life. I can accommodate."

Sir's fingernails tore into the seat's fabric. "I don't want to 'accommodate' anymore. I thought I'd left you on the barren surface of that half of Venus to die in battle. Good for you that you're safe, but we're done." He looked to his true beloved. "Koalita, she doesn't give a shit about either of us."

Mistress smiled at him—but he recognized that look in her eyes. Anger. He'd talked to someone else as if she wasn't there.

"Humans sit up the back." He climbed back down the rungs, saddened to have lost this moment to bond with Koalita.

"We'll be together forever," Mistress called to him. "Because I'm the only one you've got."

At that, Sir gasped and clambered back to the pair—but he was too late.

Mistress slung her whip around Koalita's neck. She dragged its slithering, barbed surface around, droplets of koala blood spitting out from the ensuing wound and spraying Sir in the face.

"Nooo!"

At that, the other koalas were on Mistress, chewing her flesh open. But she only cackled.

"If I can't have you—" Gnashing teeth bit her head clean off before she could complete the thought.

The koalas, whimpering, collected Koalita up, standing on her seat and raising her above their heads, singing a mournful song of healing to her.

Sir scrambled back to her, held her in his arms, cradling her to him, bawling.

"Oh, Koalita. What brave new worlds we could have shown each other."

Upon his face, he felt the stroking paws of so many of his new koala friends. As part of a famed koala ritual, each demonstrated how they collected the pain from him and placed it in their hearts. So long as he was with them, he would not suffer alone. What a wonderful gesture this was—yet performed too immediately after the source of his anguish.

"Shh." He cradled Koalita. She burbled a thin moan.

Dis came down to take in the scene. He took off his sunglasses as a mark of respect. "Sir, leave Koalita with me. I don't want to get your hopes up, but there is a chance we can save her. We have the technology on Lower Venus. Isn't that right, brothers?" He looked around.

They cried tears too profuse to consider Koalita's potential salvation. Sir looked desperately into each of their little furry faces. Sure enough, some nodded, and he heard murmurings.

"There is perhaps a way," one said. "We have done it before, for slightly less severe cases."

Dis watched as the koalas carted her towards his cockpit. "I know the ensuing time between now and when you next see Koalita will be hard for you. But I ask that you add this to the list of ways in which you trust us. I give you my assurance that we koalas will do everything in our power to ensure the speedy recovery of your beloved."

The bright future, the escape that had danced before his fingertips after the narrow escape from Upper Venus' brutal battle? Mistress rent it in two.

For all he cared, they could crumple themselves into Lower Venus' ground.

Welcome to Lower Venus

Highest emugasms per demiplanet in this corner of the visible universe!

Old lovers unwind and newcomers cum anew.

Enjoy.

CHAPTER ELEVEN

Sir's pessimistic desires of annihilation did not come to pass.

The rocket slid to the horizontal and landed on an open strip of Lower Venus' sparse and dry grasses. The koalas filed out, shielded their eyes from the sun and looked to the distance, where a thin strip of gleaming stone appeared at the end of a long motorway.

A silvery bus drove up the street to collect them. Out came a bearded human wearing a red Roman cape, gladiator sandals and a pair of brown leather briefs, in the belt loop of which was a gladius. He greeted Dis with joy, spinning him around. "Right on time! Get in, everyone, and I'll take you to the temple."

The man got behind the wheel again, and the koalas and Sir filed in.

Long enough to allow for its hundred-plus passengers, the bus returned in the temple's direction. Dis stood on the man's shoulders and massaged his neck. Sir understood this man to be Dis' boyfriend.

The landscape of Lower Venus shared many of its features with the outskirts of Earth's Athens. At the dun-coloured dirt of the roadside were men with souvlaki stands, around which sat stray dogs made lazy by the beating sun. Olive trees dropped their fruits to dry on the ground unpicked. At sporadic distances from their road were semi-eroded artefacts: statues of soldiers; the low, mosaic-laden walls of former bathhouses; the broken arches of doorways that led to nothing.

Marbled pink stone comprised the temple, which had only a single floor but was impossibly wide. Sunlight made the shallow carvings across its surface invisible, erasing all shadow.

The koalas disembarked and entered the low, arch-shaped hollow of the temple's entrance.

Many patrons within greeted them with excitement and joy. More men and women in Roman gear and their animal companions appeared, holding bunches of grapes and ornate goblets of red wine. The floor baked with the sun's heat beneath Sir's feet, entering from square holes in the temple's ceiling, creating reverent little spotlights like Heaven's rays bursting through thick clouds. The floor had mosaics like those he'd seen on their journey, and lining the room were long stone benches with angles for leaning upon.

"You're just in time," Dis' boyfriend said. "We were about to start the festivities." He clapped his hands.

A fluid, like red wine, spilt across the floor. It felt like velvet as it lapped around Sir's ankles. As it solidified, buttons appeared on its surface, separating the sections into raised diamonds. He tugged his feet out from it and walked upon the surface. It was liquid couch.

Lute and lyre players walked out of distant doorways, smiling and plucking away. A woman in a toga wheeled her harp to one corner of the room and sat upon a high bench that she found there, tuning her strings. Some of the holes in the ceiling dripped a purple goo, which lowered the room's lighting to make it more romantic. As the snakes of goo swung around, they hissed through apertures opening in their surface, which emitted a purple gas that filled the room with some aphrodisiacal, lavender-scented compound.

As the templegoers breathed in this scent, they stripped off their clothing and rubbed the surfaces of their bare skins. Women writhed on the floor, on the benches, their animal cohorts approaching them at a sultry pace.

Snakes slithered in and out of their orifices. Goats bucked at them with their horns, poking gently at their breasts. Men got hard and stroked themselves before entering those same goats.

A horny panther dug his claws into this one's shoulders and entered him as an anteater used his long tongue to worship every crevice of that one's ass.

The music of the spheres began. The room filled with the sweat and grunting of the performance, overwhelmed with koalas that joined in wherever they found an opening, invited in by all to use their double-headed organs and their mouths to pleasure and nibble however they pleased.

To Sir, this display of hedonistic abandon was empty without Koalita. He retired to the bar and watched a koala belly dancer wearily shake her hips through the floor's mess.

A barmaid looked at Sir, leaning her ample breasts on the cool marble counter. "I like your smock. I'm here informally, you know. You say the word and let's go at it."

"I can't."

He asked for a double bourbon. A naked man brought to him in a square tumbler of refrigerated marble. The man insisted on tilting the fluid into Sir's mouth and caressing Sir's throat, evidently aroused by this act.

The woman slapped her hands on the marble. "This is torture! We need permission to enter the throng, and we've never been denied." She clasped her hands together. "Please?"

Sir shook his head. The staff pouted. If Sir had asked for another drink, they would not have granted it to him. He kept his back to the orgy but heard it reach its climax as collectively, every animal moaned with greater volume until the various peaks of their pleasure dissolved.

Dis came and sat beside Sir, his Hawaiian shirt open. He politely requested a warm washcloth, which he used to clean the semen from the fur of his belly and face. He looked to Sir and grinned. "Don't worry. There will be plenty more of those for you to take part in."

"I can't think of such a thing at a time like this!"

"Well, I have good news," Dis said, placing a paw on Sir. "Reports have come back from our infirmary. Koalita has recovered. Now let's go see her."

Notice pinned to medical waste containers in the temple basement
For the last time, PLEASE start reusing cannulation needles. We don't have time to replace them between fauna switchouts if we're to make projected beast targets. Thanks—Mgmt.

CHAPTER TWELVE

Sir and Dis entered a lozenge-shaped elevator, which dropped sharply down a dark shaft. They stood side by side and looked stoically forwards. Glowing eyes on the front wall of the shaft peered at them as they passed on their descent.

"Wanna explain where we're going?" Sir threw all marks of respect for Dis to the wind. How could Dis participate in an orgy not minutes after Koalita's almost certain demise?

"Oh, it's a little project of mine." Dis had shed his Hawaiian shirt, finding it a distasteful reminder of the chastity-based slavery and departure from his beloved that he had experienced on Upper Venus. "We may have separated from our friends here, but I knew they'd keep the mission going. I don't know that I could explain it further. It's better that you witness it for yourself."

The shaft opened into a vast room, dark but for one wall, which glowed with constant fire. They still had some way to go until they reached the floor, without any safety barrier to prevent them from dropping to their certain death—but Dis stood with paws behind his straightened back, his expression resolute.

They heard low whimpering rumbling off the floor. Dim lights revealed the sheen of rows upon rows of leather chairs, extending off into the distance. They were much like Boris had in his basement. These rows began too far from the elevator for them to see what was going on until they reached the floor and walked into a weird, chilly hangar of a space.

Dis marched forwards. "I'll take you to your station."

"What? I-I wanted to see Koalita again. That's all."

"And when it comes to what's going on down here, that's all you need to worry about."

They passed by the stations. The males of many animals—an okapi, a giant meerkat, a crocodile being the first that they passed—stood in front of the chairs, onto which the females—a pig, a tiger, a pangolin in the first three instances again—lay bound.

Long plastic tubing ran from a black monolithic device at the side of each chair, connecting to central venous catheters beneath the collarbones of the males. Some bubbling purple fluid pumped into their systems. The females, too, had a catheter device, but their fluid was sluggish and pink.

"What the hell is Koalita doing in a place like this? What happens here?"

Dis approached the pangolin. "Men remain in constant heat, in musth, in all forms of sexual excitement. Women stay in a sedated grog."

The crocodile withdrew from the pangolin, panting. She was giving birth. Out came a squealing ball of a thing, with a long green mouth like its father, armoured in scales all over like his mother. The pangolin sighed. Its eyes closed. Its body twitched briefly, but the life within had snuffed out.

Koalas in white smocks and face masks approached the pangolin mother, unlatching her body and taking her away. Sir watched where they took the bodies. The fire he'd observed from the lift was a long incinerator. Silhouettes of koalas tossed the body into it. These koalas returned for the baby, which, Sir saw looking at it, had grown to three times its size. A koala stood by its side and inserted a catheter beneath its clavicle.

Dis caressed the catheter's plastic tubing. "Growth hormones. They keep the process going."

The koala attending to the former baby inspected its genitals. "Female," he said in a muffled voice through its face mask.

Dis nodded. "Strap her in then."

The koalas that had run to the incinerator returned and bound her to a chair.

From behind Sir squawked an emu. Startled, he moved out its way. The koalas pushed it into place in front of the newborn, which was now adult size. They guided the chemically hypnotized crocodile onwards to its next host—the product of the tiger and meerkat's copulation—and connected him up to the new booth's plastic tubing.

The crocodile fucked the newly strapped-in beast.

Dis looked to Sir. "Like musical chairs, no?"

"You're making an army of hybrid males!"

"To take over the universe."

Sir turned to run. Koalas swarmed him, covering his eyes and bringing him to the ground, kicking him in his side with their steel-toed boots. He cowered in the fetal position as they kept kicking. This acted as enough of a distraction for them to stab him in the neck and affix him with a mobile catheter of sedatives. This kept him subdued long enough until they could take him to his respective booth.

"Now, won't you help us?" Dis took Sir's hand and helped him back up.

"Heeeeelllpppp uuussss." Sir staggered forwards.

Sir saw, through hazy vision, a brown bean of a thing. It was bandaged Koalita, listless, plugged into the monolith's heady hormone mix.

Dis' voice muffled as if it came from the end of a fur-lined tunnel. "You know, my boy, we hope one day to make the monobeast of pure pain, the being whose conception so irked your friend Boris. Such a creature, so riled by its very existence, would no doubt act as the ultimate biological weapon, don't you think?"

"Thaaaaat's niiiiice—UGH!"

The koalas connected him to his booth's catheter. His body flooded with sex. Aggression. The rage of the hunt and the desire to celebrate its spoils. The koala in front of appeared with overwhelming lucidity! What a rush!

He growled and beat his chest, stroking his body all over. His skin drenched with the ardent desire to fuck.

"What do you say?" Dis stood back as Sir performed an impromptu war dance. "Care to help us out?"

Koalita, sedated, pleaded at Sir with her eyes. Her groggy mouth opened. "Please."

He licked his lips and laughed. "Sorry, Koalita. That sweet lemony koala pussy is too good to pass up."

DINOSAURS OF THE CYBERVATICAN:

Who is Your True Believer of Science?

Chapter One

Xakrin stood before the spermship's panoramic visor as it approached Earth.

The CyberVatican's diamond dome, atop one of the Earth's space elevators, appeared like a behemoth cat o' nine tails whipped about aimlessly by a bitter world. The little chained ballmouths around its perimeter chomped hungrily at their local vacuums. They babbled nonsense to themselves in individual godless languages until their eyeless heads sensed the ship's approach and chomped their way towards it.

Xakrin pulled his overcoat tighter over his slick and bulbous body. The material soaked up the slime that coated his surface. He wasn't used to wearing clothes, but it was the done thing on Earth at least. As for how things were in the CyberVatican, he didn't yet know.

He pondered this new venture while looking below at the old buildings within. They'd been hollowed out and fitted with metallic, sentient interiors. The parabolic shape of the un-bombed parts of the city themselves formed part of some big, decaying jawbone. The jawbone of a caveman who left no valuable clues, whose entire life and long-gone purpose remained a mystery.

The ballmouths gripped the ship, their chains retracting slowly. A docking bay dilated open like a pupil in the dome's centre. Now it was a milky eye, focusing on Xakrin and the other tourists.

The sperm entered the pupil. A multilingual message streamed across the ship's LED display: *Welcome to the CyberVatican.*

After rifling down a diamond tunnel, the ship arrived at the welcome centre. The swollen appendage of the ship's tadpole body opened and deposited the guests in a brightly lit chamber of white marble, a bastardized Panathenaic Stadium-type structure with long benches curving around the room.

The roof cranked back on hinges revealing the night. In floated Benedict Popebot v 16.0. Screaming fireworks shot out of the tubes lining his hovering throne.

This disturbed Xakrin. His Martian senses fired floods of electric potential to his core, which sang "Danger! Danger!" to him in his native tongue.

"Typical Terran display of insensitivity," he muttered to himself.

He turned around to see that spring-like Saturnians, bloated Neptunians and assorted Intersolar scum freely misted and powdered the room with scents and compounds of awe, much like Earth's own demented seahorses shooting their young into the ocean. None of them even seemed bothered that the long-awaited Popebot Francis hadn't graced them with his presence.

Steel pods hovered in over the rows of benches. They flowered open their metal petals and deposited a stream of nunbots. The bots clanked their way along in rows of decreasing numbers towards the visitors. There were ten at the top, then nine, then just one nun on the ground floor. All gyrated simultaneously. They performed the welcome dance in parental-guidance mode, but their motions more than suggested the city's seedy underbelly. This was usually kept under wraps—but what was a bit of tawdry titillation between hosts and clientele?

The dance culminated in the nuns coming apart, the flat surfaces of their bodies expanding out on extendable cords from their carbon steel bones, turning them into glowing balls that rolled around the room.

A short human man in a turquoise polo and khaki shorts emerged from a previously hidden doorway in the marble steps. He flung his arms up, and the balled women electromagnetically propelled themselves skywards, burning their baggies of metal filaments, sending a fiery golden shower over the awestruck tourists.

"Hello and welcome to the CyberVatican!" the man said. "History, secrets and many a 'Wow!' await you lucky folk. I'm Gary, your human guide through the city of original sin! Can I get a 'Heaven yeah'?"

Aliens responded with an awkward array of delayed, mistranslated speech.

When the dance was over, the nuns mingled with their guests, flinging colourful paper leis around whatever most closely resembled a neck in their targets. They handed out scrunchies with Mother Teresa's face printed on them, and boxes too small to have any evident use other than for the mild amusement of the Jesus hologram affixed to their lids. When you tilted the boxes, the eyes of a fake blood-soaked actor, hired from some Halloween costume model agency, opened and closed.

One of the nuns tried to peer beneath the wet brown flaps that covered Xakrin's Martian eyeslits. He thought her expression particularly listless. Even with fusion reactors in their cores, some of the nunbots couldn't muster the energy to smile.

She flung a lei around Xakrin's neck. It comprised severed human penises, a leftover from some warlady's bachelorette party. No matter to him. He would happily snack on the garment later, and were any of the nunbots adept at reading Martian moods, they'd know that their attempted cheer was no match for his bitterness.

Gary led Xakrin and the rest to Stage Zeta at the back of St Peter's Casino, where scheduled fun awaited. He climbed on the stage and fiddled with a gunge-coloured box. Tourists formed a circle in front, which awkwardly rose and fell over the room's slot machines and red velvet high chairs. Lunarian ratmongrels conversed with blue Venutian labiafolk. Overexcited asteroids wept mercury that scattered across the carpet. Humans made the mistake of trying to pet the burning skulls of Mercurians, thinking it uncouth to flinch, pretending not to notice the way they sizzled their skin.

Xakrin quickly found the bar and ordered a drink from the sentient saxophone bartender. Whatever he'd picked was bubbling, burgundy and served in a comedy-sized crack pipe of a container. He held the stem of it beneath his noseflap, inhaling its sweet and dry ice-like effervescence. He looked to the stage. Gary's erect, bus-shaped gunge device was a karaoke machine.

An enormous clitoris-like being cooed and approached the stage. Unfortunately for Xakrin, Martians were slow drinkers, their initial few stomachs too small for more than a few drops. He was locked in for a rendition or two of Sabrina Salerno's posthumously intergalactic smash, "Boys Boys Boys."

During rendition number three, Xakrin got up, abandoning the last third of his drink, and made for the front door. He felt a little hand slap down on him from behind.

He turned around and said, "What you might call 'the left shoulder" is particularly sensitive in Martians."

"I-I meant no harm." It was tour guide Gary. As he spoke, he was unable to stop from grinning, both rows of his bleached teeth jutting out. "I was just wondering where you might be off to tonight? We have a big day planned tomorrow."

"What farking business is it of yours?"

Gary held his hands up in surrender. "Of course, of course! Guest satisfaction is our number one guarantee! It's just sometimes we encounter clients who think they know how to satisfy themselves better than we do. In those instances, it's my responsibility to step in and say, 'Hey...?' That's when you say your name."

Xakrin's eyebrow rippled. He turned for the door again.

"I know where you're going," Gary said. "I saw the way you were looking at those nuns. You still have some of their filings orbiting your head. At least let me—"

Gary reached out to clear the halo-like rings that had gathered around Xakrin's head during the welcome dance.

Xakrin stopped him. "Leave an old perv to his business." He flopped away on the gaudy, stained casino carpet.

The floor of St Peter's Square was a giant metal LP, which rotated in sections, clockwise one way, anti-clockwise the other. Dotted around it were homeless humans and animals that, since the CyberVatican adopted Italy's idea to legalize public masturbation, spent their days jerking it until open sores coated their genitals.

Flyerbots spun around day and night, dispensing and begging and bothering. Neo-devouts wandered around in black robes, handling the city's remaining precious books with old Mickey Mouse gloves they'd had flown in specially by SpaceX. Ships—shaped like jellyfish, crosses, herons, eyeballs and other meaningless Terran objects, as was the current Intersolar trend—floated about outside the dome. Cicada-like drones buzzed around inside.

The cool metal of the disc soothed Xakrin's froggy feet. Its chill spread through the primitive nervous system of his lower limbs.

"Hey there, Mr Martian," said a metal mannequin covered in glowing, colourful hoops. "Looking for a good time?"

"You know I'm a Martian, huh?" he said. "What gave it away?"

The mannequin simply repeated its pre-recorded line.

"Hm," Xakrin took one of the metal credit cards that it dispensed. He slapped his wet feet across the square, badly timing his disembarkation from the disc, landing in the darkest alley.

"Welcome to Blib's Parlour of Putas!" said an alien of unknown origin, a stick insect-type in a greasy-looking Hawaiian shirt and wayfarers. "You want it, they do it! Conversation, massage, happy, sad, or even twist ending! Limb fiddling, cyberdick diddling, I got the finest bots in the galaxy! Now hey." He patted his chest with his forelimbs. "I've been to the coolest comets, the easiest exoplanets, the gassiest giants and lemme tellya you will not find the range of suction settings, the programmed roleplay acting skill or more genuinely configured empathyometers in this or any other universe! I see in your eyes that you were once an honest gent. So, for an extra thousand baht, I'll give you the ultra-premium rapport package. That's right, for a price, my girls will even look you in the eyes during! Don't say Blib ain't generous. And sure as fark don't take your business elsewhere! Now, what can I do for you?"

"What does this get me?" Xakrin gripped the mannequin's card between the slick webs of his three fingers.

"Nice work, man! Picked yourself up a voucher! But lemme see this one for a moment—"

Xakrin, an experienced traveller, concealed it in a palm and held it to his chest.

"What's the problem, man?" the insect said. "I have to check the colour strip on the back to make sure your card's still valid."

"Didn't you see me take it from the stand in the square?"

"Yeah, sure!"

"Then I get a discount."

"It depends what colour the strip is. Maybe you can just tell me—"

"What colour's valid at the moment?"

"What colour's your card?"

Xakrin's mouth flap rippled as he released a frustrated burst of methane. His eyebrow undulated. He noticed a being leaning on an ionic column. It smoked from a long spout that curved out the front of its head.

Xakrin pushed Blib aside and padded along the alley's glassy blue cobbles, which gave beneath his caustic feet like some weird jelly.

The leaning creature stood beneath little balls of neon that floated peacefully around him. An LED sign to one side flashed crude images of the year's most commonly sought after genders, genitals and races.

Without looking at Xakrin, he addressed him in a grinding, melancholic version of English. "You want nuns?"

As he said "nuns", a dozen or so booths lit up in blood-red light. Inside, there they were, dancing with at least an extra ten percent more hip thrust and thigh spread than they had demonstrated in the welcome dance. The lights along the booth now flickered in jazzy patterns: Mexican wave, odd and even, all flashing at once.

Xakrin's eyestalks took a three-sixty journey around his head. "How much?"

"You work that out down below."

Xakrin looked down in surprise as streetlips swallowed him up and sent him down one of the city's many oesophagi.

He slid along the cool aluminium floor of a long, dark corridor. The only light came from the sheen of partitions between its many booths. They gleamed like metallic fish ribs, away and into the darkness.

It seemed, as he listened, that every creature in the universe emitted the same sexual moan.

Oh, oh.

Uh, uh.

It was an essential feature, it seemed, that it sound animal, aggressive, base, as if it interrupting it meant death. Or worse, lifelong embarrassment. Intercourse, and maybe even its simulated, single-participant versions, were life's top priority.

Xakrin assumed the clientele were purely male. Even so, the vessels in his multi-headed ball of Martian penises distended with joy. Joy on the men's behalf, probably.

He tugged at his overcoat to keep it tighter as his genitals expressed themselves further. He continued waddling, careful to avoid the puddles of multi-coloured ooze that seeped along the corridor. Teeth-lined grates in the floor gulped welcomingly at the many fluids that spilt down their long necks.

He eventually walked by a free booth. Even better, he later found a locus of booths with no customers around. Martians were known for their love of privacy.

Placing his hand on the glass, a display appeared, declaring that by the figure in his bank account alone, he was considered a valued customer.

"Please state what you are looking for," the display said. "Pornographic show in situ? Dance? Massage? Private room? New feature, the take-in menu! Order nuns to your hotel room in as few as thirty minutes."

"Private room," Xakrin said.

An enormous chainsaw-looking thing sped out the darkness at full pelt. Xakrin flinched, but as the object rose to the ceiling and spotlights turned on along its rim, the nuns hanging from it appeared. An electronic rack allowed the user to choose his mate for the evening.

"I am Mother Ta Please Ya," the first model said.

Mother's synthetic skin was smooth and shiny. Her mirrory habit was without a fingerprint. The range of her facial expressions was impressive. The others, to her left and right, looked worn-out and cheaper.

"CerebroLock rescued my brain from the war-torn planet of Grisktuth. My irradiated, tumour-ridden body was stalking the streets in search of scraps at the time. I was eternally grateful that they found me." She pressed a hand to her chest mechanically. 'Before my mandatory computerized education, our CerebroLock's top evaluators noted that thanks to the survival skills I developed on Grisktuth, I already possessed a high degree of sexual adeptness. That's why they named my patented move The Cherry on Top."

Xakrin selected "Display Features" from the screen in front.

"Note my genitals." She pulled her kimono open and gestured to a pink ball of putty between her legs. "Provided you join me tonight from within the solar system, they're fully adaptable to accommodate your own organs. Made from SexyPutty, the mold can slide across my surface with the assistance of motile, sub-dermal harnesses to service you with the greatest of pleasure and ease. With my cold fusion core, I'll keep you up all centureeee!"

Her grin, which exceeded the width Xakrin had seen on any live human, made him shiver. He swished an arm in front of him.

The subsequent hanging nun appeared. Its facial features were not as detailed. Instead, they emerged from a board of pins, like one of those toys kids play with by making impressions of various body parts. Her eyes and lips were made from tungsten coils that transmitted emotions in the form of heat and light.

"Hi!" she said, waving. "My name is Have At 'Em Eve. My host was a virginal female being from the 'Vatican itself. CerebroLock rescued the upper half of my simple, peasant girl body from the war. You can take the brain out the virgin, but you can't take the virgin out the brain! My meek and mild-mannered nature is perfect for all of your dominant fantasies. That's why my patented move is White-Hot Mercy-Pleading Eyes of War-Torn Sadness."

Xakrin approved her. A voice asked if he would like to add more girls to his evening's entourage. Well, that was an idea. With enough bank to back it, he could use the time to pick a favourite with whom to spend the rest of his trip.

He flicked through the remaining models. Some were mangled plastic things with tentacles and rusty spikes sticking out of them. One, known as Francis the Sissy, was sopping with alien pleasure fluids. He was the only male on the rack, after all.

In the end, Xakrin selected Mother, Eve, and three further women of intermediate quality.

The glass before him slid out the way and an escalator appeared from out the floor. This carted him up to his designated bedroom.

The escalator deposited him in a room lined with red velvet. Disembodied tongues poked through the walls and licked at the air. In the centre was a large bed, purple silk sheets across its surface billowing and heaving with the room's breath. Xakrin's selected nunbots reclined on the sheets, flicking their habits seductively.

Eve approached him and gently slipped a finger of each hand beneath his eyebrow flap, looking into his eyes.

"So sad, Mr Martian," she said. "You want us to help with that?"

"He doesn't like it when the product talks." Mother was notably more acerbic now that she wasn't in factory mode on the rack.

Eve's glowing eyes conveyed her substantial jealousy of the rich mosaic of pieces in Mother's face. These could be manipulated into a variety of expressions. The other models had only motile eyebrows that tilted over a Japanese Noh mask.

"Sir," Mother continued, "wouldn't you like a go at my ever-malleable vagina?" Slipping out of her kimono, she revealed the ball of pink putty. "Please, if you will."

She motioned for Xakrin to remove his overcoat.

He peeled it off.

"Hmmm." She rigidly auto-tuned her way through several notes. Lasers surrounding the putty of her genital module scanned Xakrin's body, registering him as a Martian. He looked to Eve, and the ball of finger-like appendages around his stomach expressed themselves. Mother's putty invaginated itself in perfect counterpoint to Xakrin's sexual structure.

"Dance for him," Mother said to the other nunbots. "It's what he paid you for."

The girls danced. The velvet walls lapped at them and muffled their awkward whirring.

"Come, now," Mother said. "You'll enjoy it more from the comfort of your bed."

The bed puffed noxious gases into the room.

Mother lay Xakrin on his side. Her putty playfully rippled. His prickball reached out hungrily. Its puckering holes, like udders, ached to get their milk drained.

Harnesses moved her genitals around to meet his. Sure enough, each dick found its pussy, locking Xakrin and Mother into intercourse. The other girls got closer, caressing Xakrin's wet body. Their frail little robofingers rubbed the warts that covered his brown surface non-judgmentally. The other nunbots' function was so limited now. Mother had made sure of that, determined to remain the star *puta*.

Xakrin's mouth flap opened wide, making a quarter gap in the ball that was his head. He emitted a low and guttural sound like some unholy didgeridoo.

"Aawwwwww."

The flap widened. His head compressed further upon itself like the hood of a soft-top car disappearing, making a gaping hole of his neck.

Mother's putty vibrated with ferocity, jigging his many dicks this way and that. She made little openings in herself to siphon the alien sperm out of him with dentist-like suction tubes.

Usually, that would be that. The spent client would shuffle back onto the seedy streets, off to whatever hovel he came from. But this time, all the girls bore witness to something they'd never seen before.

From Xakrin's neck opening came a searing hot clear glass bubble. A spiky blue-hot fire inside blinded them all.

Xakrin appeared before a large cardboard building. Its window frames were made of some creamy card, its windows simply white paper.

He turned the door handle, a scrunched up ball of paper, and entered the house.

The inside looked like a burning barn with a charred floor that glowed with cinders. Its wooden beams ablaze.

At the back of the barn, beyond the brittle floorboards, there she was. His Desired.

She lay in a lacquered coffin, which was in the ovoid shape traditional for Martians. Her listless, dehydrated corpse screamed like a pissed-off frog.

Before he could approach, the floor gave beneath them, sending them to the lava pits below.

CHAPTER TWO

Xakrin woke up to a sizzling sound.

Mother was above him, forcing him to swallow the glassy pearl that he and other Martians emitted when trying to channel loved ones.

"Hey!" Mother was back in her kimono, genitals stored away safely in self-cleaning mode. "You've been here all night. We're starting to get bored. More importantly, your cash is about to run out."

"Wha?" Xakrin looked to a screen on the wall that had emerged from the wall's red velvet curtains. It counted down his money. He had another five minutes before blowing all his savings.

"You want us to take you back to the surface?" Mother said.

"P-Please," Xakrin said.

"Is he okay?" Eve came forwards from the throng of bots and placed the cool steel of her hand on Xakrin's forehead.

"He's broke is what he is." Mother walked over to the screen and made a neck-slicing motion. Their session had ended.

"You kept him here on purpose," Eve said. "You told us to stand back, that it wasn't safe to wake him. Now he's about to max out his card and you're forcing that thing back inside him like it's no big deal!"

"Why do you think you're here, missy?" Mother said. "To fall in love?"

"I don't know."

Gears on the outside of their room cranked them upwards. Eventually, they surfaced beside the light display of nuns Xakrin saw the night before. But it was time to simulate the day. Sunlight shone from the dome above.

Xakrin waddled out and onto the pavement, where he stood in front of his tour group.

Gary pointed over his shoulder—directly at Xakrin, though he didn't know. "It's critical that you don't come to this kind of establishment at night," he said. "It can be very dangerous. You never know what creatures await down these side streets."

He walked backwards into Xakrin.

The group tittered with a needling insidiousness. The springing Saturnians lingered their bounces to gawk at him for longer.

As Gary passed Xakrin, he patted his shoulder and slipped a piece of paper into an outer pocket.

"Back in the box, ladies," Mother said. "We've gotta plug in and get recharged in time for the daytime clientele. God knows what those lonely pervs are about to put us through."

"One second." Eve walked towards Xakrin.

Mother rolled her eyes and started the descent sequence without her.

"You should get back," Xakrin said.

"Hey!" Mother called as their room descended. "Know what we call Martian pervs? Multi-choded Toads! Ahaha! Multi...? Oh, whatever!"

"I was concerned." The worm-like metal coils that formed Eve's lips contorted. "Where exactly did you go last night?"

"I was just looking for something."

"Did you find it?"

"I don't—maybe I shouldn't have been looking anyways."

"I don't know why, but I want to help you." Eve rubbed one of her arms self-consciously. She was programmed to do so as a coy ploy, but it seemed genuine. She printed out a ticket from the dispenser above her left breast, tearing it off and handing it to him. "Here's my card."

"Didn't you hear what Mother said? I don't have any money left."

She smiled. "This one's on me."

"I don't know what you want," he said, "but, here, take these." From beneath a stomach flap, he dredged out a necklace of shells from Martian beaches, threaded on a string of his wife's hair.

"This is—very generous." Eve's face didn't convey this as she balled the necklace up and put it in a flap in one of her buttocks. "Catch you later."

She went to the entrance Xakrin had used to reach the corridor of pervs the night before and slipped into the ground.

Xakrin looked at the card and snorted. The model of naivety they'd chosen for the Eves was certainly endearing, but too much so. Perhaps he'd suggest CerebroLock improve her in the next revision. He filed the card away in the wet inner pocket of his coat just in case, and headed back for the square.

The morning's LP was limestone and turned only in one direction. A needle, comprised of the former Vatican's obelisk suspended by a crane, screeched out a classical rendition of Corona's "Rhythm of the Night." This made quite an inappropriate soundtrack for Xakrin's discovery, the body of a dead priest.

It was badly smashed and had clearly fallen from the surrounding curved walls. Xakrin looked up and shielded his eyeflap from the sun, trying to spot any evident clue. Just the looming shadowy formations of the statues all around—except there!

A figure dashed from behind one of the statues and away, obscured by the wall's rim. Xakrin looked at the body. Its cassock was torn open, revealing the deep gouges of claw wounds all over.

"Tragic, isn't it?"

Xakrin turned around.

It was Benedict Popebot, sitting in something like a floating metal egg. He drummed his clicking metal fingertips together, face frozen in a cruel rictus.

"Sure," Xakrin said.

"Since diversifying from our city's original source of income, not all the priests have adapted to the functions it now performs, you see. Indeed, we've had a number of casualties." His various contraptions whirred as a sad hand fell across his brow. "How I wish I could pass on my faith to the rest of the priesthood! Now that our beloved 'Vatican has fallen on such hard times, we need it more than ever. Excuse me."

He pushed Xakrin out the way with his hovering saucer. A hatch beneath the egg opened. The 'pope lowered himself over the body, his smile unfaltering as some ravenous beast within the egg devoured the body.

"Let's not go scaring the other tourists with this. And if you don't want to get further involved in this kind of mess, stick with your tour group at all times."

With that, he flew back up into the sky and darted off at the speed of light, disappearing with a "ting!" into the electric sky.

Xakrin slipped a hand into his pocket and took out the greasy sliver of paper that Gary had passed to him in secret: *Underground@Sistine. Midnight. Tonight.*

Before the war that exiled the 'Vatican from Earth, a renegade team of art historians buried the Sistine Bunker beneath the compacted dirt and rubble of the old city, protecting it from harm. Later, they drilled a tunnel through its roof, allowing access once again.

After an unproductive day of pissing his remaining money away on the slots, Xakrin climbed down a ladder at the back of the former chapel. He soon spotted Gary up the front, kneeling and praying.

Xakrin walked up beside him, keen not to interrupt.

"There is something unholy going on in the CyberVatican," Gary said.

"Everyone knows that," Xakrin said.

"I don't mean the nuns! This is far worse. Oh, we have made a false idol, and now God will punish us."

The walls of the bunker pulsated with disappointment, rippling out a rumble.

"You need to see it for yourself." Gary stood up. He to meet Xakrin in the eyes. "It's in the basement of the casino. When we face the sun, a tunnel will open beneath the stage. Crawl in and speak the following phrase: 'Abyssus abyssum invocat.'"

"Why are you telling me any of this? Why should I do it?"

Gary took Xakrin's slippery mitt in his hands. "You're not like the others. You may have been the first to leave the pack—but they were all at it later. Jovian couples bedding nunbots together. Uranian husbands betraying their wives who betrayed them in turn. Everyone wants a piece of the action." Gary caressed Xakrin's wet face with the back of his hand. "But you came here on a different mission."

Xakrin stepped back. "What is it with everyone talking about this shit all the time? I didn't come to talk. I came to cum! Aren't we over all this 'Vatican secret bullshit?"

The walls pushed inwards, claws scraping across their malleable surfaces from beneath.

Gary looked up in fright. "I've said too much already! They know I know!"

Chandeliers swung about. Paint flaked off of The Creation of Adam above, revealing, behind God, a detailed cross-section of the human teste.

"A sign!" Gary screamed. He ran to the altar, opening up a panel in the floor's stone and climbing into a passage.

Xakrin ran back to the ladder and headed up to ground level, scuttling through the streets and back to his hotel room at St Peter's Casino.

Xakrin was pleased to find everything in his hotel room set up as requested. The bed was a wide Jacuzzi covered by a purple silk sheet, which bowed and soaked into stagnant tonic water. It would help to keep his flesh cool and wet after days of reckless boozing.

The specially imported Martian chests of drawers that Xakrin had paid for in advance looked like upright pill boxes carved from soapstone. White bathroom tiles no bigger than a square inch covered the floor. A shallow pool of nutritive Martian mountain sap spread across them.

"You've been planning this for a while." Eve pulled back the Jacuzzi's silk sheet, revealing herself.

"One last blowout," he said.

He walked to his chest, pulling back one of the climate-controlled drawers. A series of live Martian slugs cried out to be fed. They were the approximate shape of a cube with rounded edges, a milky turquoise, their many mouths opening and resealing at random. Xakrin held one up. He removed a bucket of cool, rough stones from a second drawer. He dropped a few onto the slug. It opened up to let the stones fall into its liquor. Xakrin took a sip. "What exactly do you think you can do for me?"

Eve sat on the rim of the Jacuzzi and spread her legs wide. Her primitive yet seductive genital module rotated, its eight soft lips opening gently like the time-lapse of a rosebud in the sun.

"How long do you think that help lasts?" he said.

"Please." She spoke in a badly auto-tuned voice. "I know it does more than please you. The other tourists, they aren't freaks like you. The Plutonians are frigid, the Saturnians scopophobic. The Uranians don't even like a quick fingering. To name but three."

"I get what's going on. This is some scam you set up with the other Eves. It's a routine of yours."

She closed her legs again. The petals of her genitals flapped on her inner thighs in an attempt to stimulate themselves. "The other Eves? I'm the last one! Clients broke all the rest." Eve folded her arms. "You don't know how lucky you are, do you? Well, I do. I know you'd never treat me that way."

They were silent for a moment, looking in opposite directions.

It was dark again. Through the large contact lens-like surface of the space elevator dome, beyond its hazy radiation shield, some metal trapezoid appeared against the meagre light of old stars, against the melancholy darkness.

"More of us arrive," Eve said.

The ship took on its familiar shape, a floating metal womb with ovary thrusters.

"You must be so thankful," Xakrin said drily. He was recalling the stock phrase he'd heard several times the previous night when flicking through the nunbots hanging from the rack.

"Not at all," Eve said. "You know all our backstories are—" Her face flattened to a screen. Words, written in the electric arcs of a taser, buzzed across it: *Reach behind my neck and turn the dial there until you hear a warning signal. CerebroLock can hear everything.*

He pretended to draw her in for a kiss, then turned the dial as requested.

"That's it," she said. "The warning sound is probably too high for you to register. We have five minutes to talk before they assume I can't fix the problem myself." She picked up one of his slugs, stroking it. It squealed contentedly as she spoke. "At seventy-two, I was the powerful magnate of an intergalactic uranium merchant. Business was booming, so to speak, but my anxieties about getting older were affecting my work. I bought a premium package with CerebroLock. They told me they'd download the contents of my brain and place them in a suitable android model so I could live forever. Instead, they sent me here.

They told me if I protested, if I disobeyed, they would shut me down permanently. They promised me that if I 'completed a tour', as they put it, they'd free me. That was well before the city even reached the end of its tether." She smirked wryly at this, gesturing at the surrounding stars. "I knew they'd never let me leave."

"You think I'm pathetic, don't you?" Xakrin said. "You think I'm some sad old perv who'll take you away with him, back to his home planet, to a better life. You picked the wrong toad, missy. I'll die here before that happens."

"I would've left by myself already if such a thing were possible," she said. "Proximity alarm. I'd never make it."

"What do you want, then?"

"My genital set may not allow for specified fit, but I still feel real good." Ending her spiel with this pre-programmed stock phrase, her voice raised seamlessly into its customer-attracting baby's pitch. The warts across Xakrin's flesh squirmed.

She tilted her head down and turned the dial back to its original position. "Sorry, boss," she said into a wristpiece. "Customer getting frisky."

Xakrin held her wrist gently and took her over to the bed, lowering her onto the silk sheet and into the water. He took off his coat and slopped it to the ground. Climbing on top of her, he awkwardly positioned his chodeball over the putty-like sponge that emerged from her flaps. As he thrusted, the water fizzed violently, bubbling black.

Before her head submerged and sparked, she said, "Baptise the fark outta me."

CHAPTER THREE

Xakrin stood, to his delight, in front of his wife. They stared at one another in a long misshapen corridor of white bathroom tiles, which curved downwards, the end stretching out of sight. Rooms branched off from the corridor at regular intervals.

"Bork, I—"

"You look like you're about to shit!" Bork exclaimed.

"What?"

"If you want to shit in my bathhouse, you gotta pay for it!"

His twenty stomachs, which increased in size in accordance with the Fibonacci sequence, warbled uncomfortably. "Bork, I don't know what's going on here, but I don't have any money on me."

"You don't pay with money. You pay with tokens you get at the reception!"

"Where's the reception?"

"We don't farking have one!"

'Then what am I to do?"

"I'll tell you what you'd better not do, and that's SHIT!"

As she said this, a squirt of his diarrhoea plopped onto the floor beneath him.

"Geez, I'm sorry, Bork! I just want to take you home with me!"

"Take me home with you? You just shit yourself, and you want to take me home with you? The least you can do is lick that up. Now!"

Xakrin prostrated in front of her, his ball-like brown tongue emerging and rolling across the mess. He gagged but successfully swallowed.

"Oh no!" He made a small bowl from the webs of his hands beneath his rectum and voided two handfuls of lumpy liquid shit into his hands. He looked through one of the doorways and saw a series of toilets in a row.

The toilets performed a baritone acapella piece, their porcelain mouths vibrating.

He looked back at Bork. "Please! Just let me throw this away in one of the toilets and wash my hands and I'll take you away from here!"

"Customers can wash their hands for free," she said, "but they can't dispose of any shit in my sinks. That's what the toilets are for. If you want the toilet, you gotta PAY!" She was panting from exertion now.

Martians could reach some volume if they wanted to, but Bork had never screamed at him like that. His blood ran colder. Maybe she wasn't his wife, but one of those Vision Demons that steals the form of the Desired to torment Travellers for fun. That seemed like the more likely scenario, though many others were possible.

Whatever was happening, he thought it best to play along for the moment.

He waddled, cupping the shit, which sloshed about with each step, dripping out the bowl of his fingers and down the backs of his hands. He closed his eyes hard and prayed that the drips didn't spill as he made his way into one of the rooms and over by one of the sinks. He brought his arms around his back and over his head. The bathroom mirror before him melted.

Bork watched sternly as he brought the bowl to his face and supped from it. It tasted like some delicate nutty cheese, but the Swedish fish juice smell of it was ungodly.

"Drink it up!" Bork demanded. "Drink it quickly, you disgusting mess! I'd hate for my customers to come in and see you drinking your own shit, so hurry up! It's a courtesy to you that I let you do this, so do it now and do it quickly! EAT THAT SHIT, YOU SHIT!"

"Fark!" he said. "There's no way I can do this!"

Shitvapors made the mirror melt entirely off the wall now. He couldn't see the source of the voice that now spoke to him. It could have been in his own head.

"You go, Xakrin!" it said, low and manly. "You don't need to do this! Just run, run away from her! She's not who you think she is!"

He shivered with fear, drops of shit landing in the sink. Black burn marks appeared on the porcelain where it landed. Now an alarm sounded. A beacon flashed red on the wall. Well, it was too late now anyway.

He turned and threw his shit directly into Bork's eyes, pushing past her.

"WELL I NEVER!" She ran blindly after him, pinging off the corridor walls. "I NEVER! I REALLY FARKING NEVER!" She followed him over the lip of the corridor's horizon as it bent downwards. Gravity followed, and they were still able to run on the floor as it curved to the vertical and beyond. Now they ran upside down. Occasionally glancing left and right, Xakrin saw each room's contents were exactly the same, Scooby Doo-style. The alarms in each were ringing now. The rooms slowly collapsed in size.

He took a sharp left into one of the rooms.

It was different. He'd now entered a labyrinth of showers. Turning this way and that, each row of showers branched off into more rows.

"I'll find you!" Bork shouted, fainter and fainter each time. It was an empty threat.

He was safe. At least from her. At least for now.

Xakrin had doubted anyone else was here, but he soon encountered many of the bathhouse's customers. The row of showers in front, in yet another white-tiled room, had shallow baths of a sort in front of them, with gentle ridges between them that weren't high enough to separate the water of each bath. Running showers filled the connected ten-or-so baths with milky blue water. Xakrin thought that the water was rich in minerals, which would account for its consistency. But as he saw the pile of humans writhing in it at the other end, he figured it was due to their contamination.

There were fifty or so of them in a big mountain of meat that pressed into the corners of the room, up to the ceiling. Their skins, glabrous as a baby's, white as an albino's, were tattooed with old, fading incoherent writing, once black, now blue. Tumours grew big as grapefruits through the hair on their heads, out their necks and stomachs. Some were missing legs. Others had little Thalidomide baby arms. All were engaged in an interlinked carnal pleasure.

"Welcome," moaned a young man whose lower half sunk into the waters. A lumpy genderless head bobbed over his genitals. "You've found us. You came to this specific branch of showers for our orgy, didn't you now? Well, come! Join in. I know we're all humans, but we have nothing against Martians."

"What the hell is going on?" Xakrin said.

"A little lost?" said a voice behind him.

He turned to see a bald, naked, scar-covered man who brandished a mouldy baseball bat.

The man saw Xakrin looking at the bat. "The humidity," he said, slapping the end of it in his hand. "Come with me. I'll take you where you need to go."

Xakrin followed him out of the room.

There was a blue wall before them, with two identical varnished pine doors. Their windows were caged with chicken wire.

"This is our art gallery," the man said. "We're interested in the chicken motif." He opened the left-hand door, and Xakrin followed him in.

The floor was littered with brown hens. Some were alive, others not. The man gestured to a dusty vitrine with a stuffed, headless rooster in it. A string of LEDs in a plastic cord emerged from its neck. They shone red light in a sequence to indicate spurting blood.

"Come come," the man said. "More chicken art awaits."

"More chicken art awaits!" The dead chickens sang.

The pair crunched their feet over mangled, feathery corpses.

They entered a bending strip of art gallery which, Xakrin imagined, connected up in the shape of an upright doughnut. Giant elaborate chandeliers floated, their crystals dancing, catching the light. Beyond the peeling teal walls, through the windows, was outer space. The curve of some unknown pink planet floated by, a permanent storm flashing across it.

"Look at this one." The naked man held up a flattened and laminated chicken. Barnacles covered one side. They'd been spray-painted with dots of pink, green, black and grey. "What does it mean, huh?" he held it threateningly in Xakrin's face. "What the fuck does it mean?!"

"I-I don't know," Xakrin said.

"Me fucking neither!"

"Who made it?"

"I fucking did! Now come here."

Xakrin heard a distant rushing sound, a rumbling beneath his feet. He looked over the bannister to the floor below. A thousand of the naked man's clones ran in a big, long circle.

On their walk, they passed glass displays. In the centre of each was a single orange pill with a large label in each corner that said "Chicken®."

"Okay," the naked man said. "I have just one more thing to show you. It's my favourite piece of art, and it's up here."

He disappeared into a doorway. Xakrin followed, climbing a set of cold concrete steps lit by natural light from windows at each landing. Beyond these windows was a red and white lighthouse.

As Xakrin reached the top of the stairs, his hearts sank. There were more shower heads along the teal-wallpapered walls.

"My favourite piece of art," the man said, "is where we kill you."

Xakrin ran through the room and into an adjacent set of toilets, hiding in one of the stalls and locking the door behind him.

Outside, several men in black boots walked in casually, kicking at the door.

Slam, slam.

The lock soon broke, and the door flung back.

Xakrin held his arms in front of his face

The clone men stabbed his neck repeatedly with weird shivs.

CHAPTER FOUR

"Ahhh! Ahhh!" Xakrin screamed, choking on his hot pearl.

"Hey hey hey," Eve said. "They didn't get you. You're here again. You're in the CyberVatican. You're safe."

"You saw them?"

"I watched the flames in your pearl. I learned to decode their images. That woman was your wife. She's the one you're looking for."

"It's none of your business!" Xakrin shuffled to one side of the Jacuzzi.

Eve sat at the other end. "The least you could do is tell me what you're up to."

He drummed sticky fingers on his lower lip. "Martian Vision System. It's incredibly dangerous. It leaves users prone to psychic attack. The chances of finding my Desired with MVS is like half a percent—although because of the many ways visions have gone wrong, no one can ever be sure."

"You need to fuck someone to use this system?"

"Any heightened emotion coaxes the pearl out, but pleasure is the nicest way." He hesitated before continuing. "My wife. She was home. I was out mining asteroids. Squid slaughtered her."

Eve bit her lip. "I'm not comfortable with racial slurs."

"You would be if a bunch of dirty squid ravaged your home planet. With nowhere to go, I came here. Thought I could harvest Bork's essence from the visions and bring her back in another's body." He lowered his head. "I can't do this anymore. She's gone forever."

Outside, someone screamed.

"Shit!" Eve said. "If there's some commotion outside, I can't go down there. Mother can't know I was here. I'm going out the window."

"I'll check it out."

He opened his bedroom door and looked to the casino below.

The tourists had gathered in their circle. Their eyes, or similar, focused on the ceiling.

Gary's lifeless body hung from the chandelier by a paper chain of the dick leis. A sadistic smile tore across his face from ear to ear. Solidified streams of blood ran down both inner thighs, suggesting a castration. A cardboard sign hung around his neck, a message written in blood across it: *Do the right thing*.

The cyberpopes must have discovered his plot.

Xakrin did his best not to draw attention to himself as he walked to the bar. He ordered a bong from the saxophone man and sat with his back to the body.

A pile of silvery dirt assembled beside him.

"To Gary," Xakrin said. "He died without getting his sorry little pecker wet."

"A tragedy indeed," Benedict Popebot said. "Whatever the boy was up to, he never had a chance. I certainly hope that no other being, lucky just to be alive, attempts to follow suit. Well, see you."

The dust exploded and stuck to Xakrin's face.

CHAPTER FIVE

After staff cut down the body, the posse of gawkers cleared out the casino. This gave Xakrin a clear window to crawl beneath the stage and find the opening Gary had referred to in the bunker.

Once the sun was directly above their dome, he said the password: "Abyssus abyssum invocat."

The entrance appeared.

It looked at first just like a sixteenth-century painting of Jesus lying on the floor. As Xakrin got nearer to it, he saw that it was a series of such portraits. Clear lubricant from multiple jets installed at the very top of the chain streamed down them.

He sat down on the first portrait. A series of lights turned on at either side. The slide tilted downwards. Its spiral shape deepened and Xakrin slid down over Jesus portrait after Jesus portrait.

The final incline of the slide had no barriers on either side. It spiralled in a downward cone over a spike pit of processional crosses. A true test of faith.

The lubricated flume deposited Xakrin at full force onto a pile of straw lit by a single flaming torch on the wall. He removed the torch to navigate the chamber ahead. Its holder sprung back with an ominous click.

Xakrin stood still. Nothing happened. He pressed on.

To his left and right were a collection of wooden stands, plaques with popes' names on them, and brass rods that ran up behind the skeletons of the named popes. An honourable procession of the dead in various poses. They played crazy golf, buggered a pig skeleton, self-harmed with a cleaver and shat out a dried rat.

Xakrin walked onwards through this room. The floor's slope increased until he slid into a large, circular room which had the clean, rubbery scent of a science museum.

What Xakrin discovered was far from scientific.

At first glance, the structure looked like the bones of Pope Francis, preserved here after his cybercanonization. He'd passed away not weeks before Xakrin arrived at the 'Vatican. The funeral was lavish and the 'Vaticans very first for a supercentenarian. Since everyone was still mourning, Francis had not yet been resurrected in cyberpope form. That was the official response—but ever since the funeral, the gutters of the Sistine Bunker had mysteriously begun to pour out blood-red smoke.

Xakrin passed his torch over the feet of the object in front of him. Several human skeletons comprised its structure. Its legs first bent slightly backwards like a bird's. The pelvis was several pelvises glued together into a much larger structure.

Xakrin's hearts fell as he moved the torch over to the left, showing the megaribs and giant vertebrae of the thing. He finally reached its superskull, made from mashed, dusty old bones. Human eye sockets were visible along its jawline. Stray teeth stuck out of the hollow meant to be the beast's nostrils. Smooth curves of human skulls created irregularities in the superstructure's silhouette. Some deviant had, from the exhumed bones of apparently every pope there ever was, constructed a makeshift T-Rex.

"The image of God!" Xakrin whispered.

The T-Rex turned and gave him a faceful of sleeping gas from its nostrils.

When he woke up, he felt more hay beneath his hands. But the cinderblock walls of this new chamber were much narrower, and there was no light. Feeling around, his hands brushed across a silk cape. He gripped a shoulder. Narrowing his eyeslits, he saw the body of Pope Francis.

"What are they going to do with you?" Xakrin said.

To his surprise, Pope Francis looked up at him. "They're going to kill us both."

"You're alive!"

"Not for long."

"Who are 'they'?"

"Not 'they'; I!" A voice boomed from loudspeakers high above.

Lights flooded the room, revealing a small diamond sphere attached to the ceiling, perhaps a mile up. There was a small shining dot inside, moving around.

Just above the walls was stained sandstone of a gladiator arena. Xakrin's narrow chamber was in the centre.

A circle of screens around the ceiling revealed Benedict Popebot's grimacing face.

"I'm taking back this great city in the name of CHEES-SUSS!" he barked.

Xakrin instinctively wiped his face for saliva, though there was none.

"The world has spiralled into godlessness!" He rambled on.

"Can you summarise for me?" Xakrin said to Pope Francis.

"He usurped my popehood for his own selfish gains. He's a madman. He thinks the only way to bring salvation to the people of Earth is with the Second Coming."

"The Second Coming? How does he plan to bring that about?"

Pope Francis adjusted his glasses. "Oh, but he already has! He took Jesus' DNA from our secret vault, something we would never think to tamper with. To create a new Jesus, he needed a viable host. But he made a mistake. He injected it into the wrong embryo!"

"Which embryo did he use?"

"That of—a T-Rex!"

At one end of their narrow chamber, a new set of lights revealed a bearded T-Rex in a cage. Golden crosses bedizened its white-painted hide. It roared again, baring its teeth of pure platinum.

"RUN!" Benedict bellowed. The cage door dropped to the floor.

The Jesusaurus gave frightening chase.

Francis dragged behind instantly, tripping over his robe, clipped by a practice chomp.

Xakrin, possessing an average Martian body, was a slow mover too. He kept looking forwards at the arena at the end of the cinderblock walls. His sticky body collected dirty straw from the floor as he ran. He felt the heat of the Jesusaurus' breath on his neck and jolted at the sound of its powerful jaws clamping down on themselves, assured that death would soon follow.

"Save yourself, my Martian friend!" Francis called.

Xakrin turned to watch.

The Jesusaurus deftly flung Francis in the air. Time seemed to slow as Francis flicked through his rosary beads while pirouetting with poor form through the arena's air. He muttered a silent prayer before landing back in Jesusaurus' jaws and screaming. Xakrin glanced up at Benedict's sphere in the ceiling, finding it empty. He hadn't even cared to watch.

Xakrin was off again. He ran and made it out of the chamber and into the arena itself, across its dusty stone grounds, running towards its columns, its arcades.

The Jesusaurus targeted him, the thump of its feet extra resonant on the unforgiving stone.

Xakrin balled up and rolled through one of the arcades. If he made it through its narrow entranceway, he'd be safe!

He felt a twinge of dull pain in one foot. The Jesusaurus had it in the grasp of his pointed teeth, tearing holes in his flesh as easily as poking a stake through silk. The holes wept thick, brown blood.

Xakrin tugged back, tearing the foot further, the holes wider, until the flesh was thin and stringy. Its bonds soon tore from one another like soft wax.

The Jesusaurus' roars haunted his ears. As he hobbled out the arena, through a network of dark tunnels, feeling his hands along the stony walls, he thought he could still hear it chasing him.

A yellow light shone somewhere down one of the branches. Xakrin navigated himself towards it, finding a cylindrical chamber like a well, lit from above. He stood in it and a pinball spring shot him into the sky.

CHAPTER SIX

The brief few seconds that Xakrin remained in the sky, shot out of St Peter's Square's centre, were so sweet. The sun shone over the ancient city in the distance, whose buildings proudly received the light. Their solar roofs, cyberparapets and weird new spires glinted. In different hands, the CyberVatican could have been a glorious, prosperous union of beautiful history and inspiring technology.

The scene directly beneath betrayed this. Nunbots, like skittering, metallic beetles, bolted across the square, tearing into the tourists they found there. The Saturnian springs stretched out so far that they could never hope to recover their original shape. The brittle bellies of the Jovians caved in, their chocolate-coloured blood flooding away their suspended organs. The clitoris beast slit open down its centre. Flushed with blood as always was, it bled instantly, spilling two rivers at its poles across the ancient stone.

Mother flew in before Xakrin on her saucer. She'd mummified herself in a string of alien guts, which made a squishing sound as air rushed by.

She wore a salacious look on her bronze face and spoke to Xakrin coolly. "Eve told you the whole thing, huh? That the creepy backstories we told you were fake. That we kept up the whole maiden-needing-rescued shtick at penalty of death? I was a fucking senator on my planet, Xakrin. Now I'm lucky if I get to *fuck* senators! More often I get stuck with Intersolar garbage like yourself and make money for dirtbag pimps from fuckin' nowhere nebulas!"

She slid her saucer beneath him and took him safely back to ground level.

"Look at your handiwork," she said.

Those meek nunbots he had hired out of pity, with the rusty implements sticking out their arms, thighs and heads, now pulled those objects out with glee and sliced them into creepy-but-harmless tourists.

"You know," Mother continued, "I told myself I was doing the universe a favour. If the creeps kept fucking me, they couldn't reproduce. I was, in my own way, murdering future generations of losers." Her head bobbed back and forth. "The feeling didn't last long. So I built a portfolio of regular clientele, got them into riskier and riskier shit and convinced them *they* wanted *me* to slice them up." She shook her head. "Not enough death. So now this. Get thee to a nunnery!"

She pushed him off her saucer into the fight below. For the first time, he screamed with genuine emotion. There was something he had indeed left unfinished and wanted to stick around for. His hands waved in front of him on the descent. Nuns appeared below, in a mire of metal dust, sparks and the flying limbs of so many tourists.

Splat. Like a rubber ball, he compressed into a sphere and rebounded unharmed. Something pinned him. It was one of the mannequin nuns with pink tentacles for arms. She squeezed him tightly and held up his arms from behind. He looked ahead and saw a nun whose habit of flapping mirrors made a spike formation atop her head. She rushed it directly at Xakrin's stomach.

"Nooo!"

The horror of impending disembowelment fueled his pearl. He vomited it into the air and it shone with yellow light, a blinding little sun of hope.

CHAPTER SEVEN

Xakrin held his breath.

He looked at his hands. He was in a space suit. In his palm was a flashlight, which he accidentally shone in his eyes.

He ventured forth, holding the torch in front of him. The room around him was dark and the black metal floor sloped against him as if described by Lovecraftian laws of geometry.

Something pulled him down the mountainous metal on his front.

A monolith, like a blunt black icicle, fell wearily from the ceiling and pinned one of his legs. The nervous system in his extremities was too rudimentary for this to hurt. He felt something like an immense physical blueness.

Footsteps. He heard footsteps and shone his torch in their direction. This revealed a weird, alien temple of sorts. Hand-engraved tablets in unreadable hieroglyphics. Enormous rows of alien princes on thrones so gargantuan that the torch's beam faded where it reached the princes' thorny knees.

Someone emerged from an arched doorway.

Beep, beep, beep.

"It's you," the creature said.

"I've heard that before," he responded.

It was Bork, but Bork before he knew her. Her flesh was still green and hadn't reached the earthier tones that years more of microwrinkles would provide. His torch picked up her adornments of gold wire with coloured, spherical jewels threaded upon it in galaxy-like formations. Some of them glowed ethereally, like little suns.

This vision came closest to what he desired. But it still lacked order or sense.

Had all of his MVS-fueled missions, and hence his visit to the CyberVatican, been utterly futile?

"I know you," Bork said. "You're the one I've been looking for."

"Then tell me my name!" He screamed at the vision.

"I confess I don't know it. But allow me to introduce myself anyway. I'm Bork."

"What?"

She flapped the sticky webs between her fingers. He'd known her to do that when she was nervous. When she did this, he would say, "Spit it out, love," as he did now.

She gasped. "We get married, you and I!"

"Yes!"

"Oh, Mom's gonna be so mad if she finds out I let myself have a vision. But it was so worth it. I don't know what all the fuss is about!"

She ran to him and squeezed him around his neck. His flesh compressed so that his helmet popped off. The pair paid this no mind, kissing each other all over like gleeful children at play.

"Bork, promise me you'll never do this again," he said. "Have a vision, I mean. Never even tell me you used the MVS, or that we talked."

"Give me a good reason not to." She folded her arms and stamped her feet cartoonishly.

He'd never found this as endearing as her mother had. But in this younger incarnation of his beloved, it seemed to fit.

Tears coated his eyes. "You and I are about to have the best time. And neither of us want anything to stop that from happening. I never learn that we met here, so I never can. If I do, you'll change the course of events, and I'll never get to look upon your beauty this one last time."

Just before her jewels erased the vision in a flash of green light, he saw her nodding.

CHAPTER EIGHT

Xakrin woke up coughing, feeling the sizzle of the burning pearl as Eve shoved it back down his throat.

He looked up at her. The pinpoint impression of her face revealed a flat expression of concern. "Why did you bring me back here? The nunbots are about to tear me apart."

"Look!" She rolled out of his way so he could see the scene in the square.

Albino raptors tore through sparking wires and holy circuitry. They were tattooed with gold crosses and lashed out with platinum talons.

The doll-like heads of nunbots flung upwards into the air, exploding like those fireworks they'd used to welcome Xakrin and his crew.

"It's a dinomiracle," she said.

A raptor flew over her shoulder and made straight for Xakrin's neck—but Eve whipped out Bork's necklace and strangled the little fucker to death.

"I have seen the Second Coming," Xakrin said as she helped him up. "And it's absolutely Cretaceous."

"Eeeee!" The raptors poured over the nunbots a rumbling river of wrong.

Eve's thrusters burned blue flames at her back. "Let's get you to an escape pod."

Up above, a collection of spheres budded out the diamond dome.

"No, please!" he said to Eve. "If you take me up there, you'll get fried. I've already lost one love. I can't leave another behind."

Diesel poured from the pins closest to her tear ducts. "Are you saying what I think you are?"

"I won't say it," he said. "Not if you plan to destroy yourself. I won't say something so lovely to someone who'd destroy themselves for a simple toad like me."

"Look up again," she said. "Look closer."

There was a buzzing blue laser grid beneath the diamond balls at the city's vertical limit. It curved in smaller parabolas, this way and that, across the sky. With fading strength, it tried to hold onto its power.

"The proximity grid," Xakrin said.

"It's dying," Eve said. "I can escape with you."

The Jesusaurus Rex thundered across the square and barreled into a column. Up above, one of the metal statues, usually covered with a weird, coloured lightning, toppled from its wall and shattered as it hit the ground. Chips of stone from the floor pinged in all directions.

Then came a sound like "Bowwwww." The grid fizzled, sparked, and gave in. Eve was free.

"Quickly!" Eve held her arms tight around Xakrin's squishy torso. His water snake-like consistency threatened to evade her grasp once her thrust kicked in. Soon the acceleration slowed, and they were up and away together.

Xakrin looked down at the raptor hanging from a web between his toes. When he kicked at it, the web tore open and the raptor spun towards the earth, screeching on the way down.

The eyeball-like pod dilated on their approach and accepted them willingly into its temporary housing. It registered that they posed no threat and carted them safely across the diamond membrane of the city.

"This next part's quite dangerous," Eve said, "but you have to trust me."

Xakrin nodded.

"Okay, so hold your breath!"

The diamond sphere fused with the ceiling's membrane and deposited them on its external surface.

Eve ran, Xakrin's weightless body trailing behind her. A wave of ice propagated across his face as he began his hibernating freeze. His eyebrow solidified with rigid concern.

Eve dashed towards a wombship. In the absence of travelling sound, he imagined her reassuring voice echoing through his system. He fainted, watching bursts of white light and dust firing out of the dying CyberVatican.

"Ahhhh!"

Xakrin sat up slowly. Crystals of ice within him slowed the movements of his joints. Frost across his skin prevented him from its usual ease of folding.

He lay upon the warm, blood-filled inner surface of the wombship's floor. He raised a hand. He had stuck to the womb's walls, dissolving its lining and absorbing its nutrients.

"It's best if you stay there," Eve said. She piloted the ship in front of its main window while sitting on an egg-shaped object, a biological chair of sorts. "My ship wants to heal you, let you grow."

"Where are you taking me?" he said.

Her head pivoted to look at him. In response, her lips rippled with electric arcs of lascivious pleasure.

EVERYBODY WANTS TO SAVE

SUPERMAMMAL CITY

In a recently discovered pocket of the universe was a closely-knit
collection of city-sized planets. Most of them went unnamed and unexplored. You
could see how pointless they were from afar with their earwax-coated surfaces,
their prehistoric pits of molten latex, or that one furthest away from all of
them that was, for whatever reason, in the shape of Grace Jones' head as it
appeared on the cover of her album *Slave to the Rhythm*.

 Amongst the semi-useful were The Palace of Lost Keys, Infinite Train
 Loop, Frozen Coffee Wasteland, Do You Like These Trees?, Hangnail Valleyville,
 Bitch Island—a resort planet with the slogan "Population: You!"—and Supermammal
 City, the planet on which our story begins.

WEIRD FAUNA OF THE MULTIVERSE

A little nobody named Bobbie wandered down some forgotten grimy alley, looking, innocently enough, for a recycling station. Instead, he found a slop of sentient toxic sludge, which now ate through his lower extremities.

The sludge growled, its epic maw engulfing Bobbie up to the upper thigh.

Glowing secretions burbled out its innermost sacs, their warm enzymes chewing steadily through his clothes. Like shells to a snail, barrels rolled on the undulating waves of the sludge's back, sickly yellow eyes emerging from its face as it absorbed Bobbie's power. Sparkles gleamed out its green goop and shone a grim path through the labyrinth of alleys. Yet Bobbie wore an expression of mild inconvenience, boredom even.

"Oh, no," he said into his phone, which fell to the floor in front of him. The Super app spun a yellow disc on the phone's touchscreen surface, recording the nature of his complaint.

Munch, munch. His waist disappeared into the beast's mouth. But then he heard a familiar whooshing above. He rolled onto his back to look up at the sky and see who he'd managed to summon.

Hugh was first on the scene, announcing himself as always with a trail of vomit. His feline body misted his way across the sky and he filled the alley's air with his alkaline stink.

"Never fear." He floated down to the ground, underestimating the upthrust required to land successfully, falling to his knees into a black puddle.

"The Wee Jakey is here!"

"Aw, man!" Bobbie said. "The Wee Jakey? I thought you were dead."

"Thought I was...?" Hugh scoffed. "I'm your only hope of salvation, big man! Keep quiet while I—bleeeeeuuurghhh!"

Milky sick coated his furry black chops. He wiped away the mess with a paw. His cape of purple suede remained unsicked, but it sopped up the puddle's water and would need a good dry cleaning. Hopefully, his wife would spot it.

Blackouts claimed his memories most nights.

Hugh staggered towards the slime. It roared and chomped on Bobbie, swallowing him up to the waste. Purring with conviction, Hugh began a rhythmic hiccoughing. A bionic furball was imminent.

"Fear not!" Ms T.N.T said. She landed in her liquorice-red lace-up boots with a slight stagger, staring into her phone the whole time. With one final *bang* from the explosive capsules strapped to her tail, she steadied herself, sliding her phone back into her utility belt and collecting a pawful of explosive beads, ready to launch at the slime.

Bobbie rested an elbow on the gritty asphalt and watched them impatiently.

"Back off, Katya!" Hugh said. "This one's mine."

"Stand back!" Ms T.N.T.—"Katya"—said. "I'm about to blow this slime sky high."

"Fear not!" said the Lavender Pusses, Pete and Geoff. Both their spandex suits collected an airstream that rippled the material with a gentle, continuous farting sound as they approached. "We came as soon as we got the signal," Pete said.

"We sure did!" Geoff said.

"Fear not!" Chromium Dominic said, sliding in on the flying saucer his feet made when he clipped them together. Their two canoe-like shapes separated as he landed, the little square mirrors of his cape blinding the

gang as it
blew in the breeze.

"Fear not!" Nuke-Pants hovered in with the power of his pants, his goat's
hooves crunching on Dominic's cape to Dom's evident irritation.

"Fear not!" Unusual Infection Susan propelled herself towards the alley
with jets of black pus.

"Fear not!" Latisha Banana walked into view, unzipping the banana peel
she was found in in that field thirty years ago.

Hugh pinched the bridge of his nose with two claws. "Okay, well, here we
are again. I don't know what anyone expected. How do you propose we resolve
this?"

"I need this win!" Katya said. "I can't go back to my husband
empty-handed. I can't take that mockery anymore. Have some compassion, please."

"To be honest," Pete said, "we're not in a good place either."

"Pete!" Geoff said.

"Well, it's true!"

"You think I'm holding you back, don't you?"

Pete held his husband's face in his paws. "What did I do to make you
think that? What can I do to make you feel good about yourself again?"

"I'm not a well cat," Hugh said. "One more failure is all it'll take to
push me over the edge."

"My pants are going to explode any day now," said Nuke-Pants, the
rectangular slits of his goat pupils widening with fear. "Then what am I to do
for work?"

"Chromium is not immune to corrosion, you know," Dominic said. "You
think I'm just going to carry on like this forever. That's not the case!"

"Rrreow!" Pete yowled, to break up their bickering.

They all turned towards him.

Pete and Geoff had dragged Bobbie from out the slime, which subdued into
a serene pink, dotted with patches of soporific purple crystals.

It snored, bubbles of gas bursting through its surface with each exhalation.

"This is ridiculous." Bobbie unpicked globules of snot-like secretions from his jacket and jeans.

Hugh ran up to him and clawed at his legs. "You're gonna write up that we were all here, though, right?"

The alley began to unpack its supermammals. They flew back into the dusk's orange sky, floating away.

"Oh sure," Bobbie said to Hugh. "I'll write it up for you. Write up that you were all a reeeeal fuckin' help. Couldn't have survived without you!" He got up and walked off out the alley, muttering.

Katya sighed. "We can't carry on like this."

"Quit, then!" Pete said. "We're the ones who actually did something anyway."

"You all stole my prize!" Hugh said. "I was first on the scene. Don't any of you have integrity?"

"You wanna talk about integrity?" Katya said. "How many paws am I holding up? The market is saturated, Hugh, and I say this with love—you've got to get it together. You *were* one of the best the city had ever seen. But after your performance today?"

They stood in a loose square, looking to each other, not sure what to say. Geoff broke the silence, weeping as quietly as he could. Pete licked at the ginger ruff of fur around Geoff's neck affectionately.

"I love all you guys so much," Geoff said. "Please don't fight."

"There's gonna be more villainy," Pete said. "There's been a slump for a few years, but that's how this industry goes! It goes around in cycles. The villainy grows and peaks and everything looks grim. We rush in and vanquish it, and now we're back in a trough of peace. We've seen it time and again."

With all due respect, Pete," Katya said, "I don't think that's what this is."

Hugh's little shoulders slumped. "The heyday's over. Supermammals aren't the new black anymore."

Pete shot them an angry look and continued to stroke Geoff's fur as he cried. But the look in his eyes wavered. He couldn't refute what they said. It wasn't their responsibility to assuage the truth for his husband.

"Okay." Hugh looked into his phone. He couldn't see a single cry for help. "That's all for this evening."

CHAPTER TWO

Back in his Upper Gingerbelly flat, Hugh looked out his window at the wistful night's stars, at the curvature of the cities that populated the distant sky. All the local planets that shared Supermammal City's solar system were, like SMC itself, single locales that wrapped all the way around their planets' surfaces. The Matchstick Head, The Supermarket of Quality Foodstuffs and Old Videogame Cartridge Quarry were all close enough to observe from SMC. The rough, jagged peaks of the buildings on these planets' surfaces looked like a ferrofluid drawn outwards in every direction.

A biobulb buzzed by Hugh's window, floating through the streets in its preconfigured pattern. Its bioluminescent cells held in a network around internal bubbles of gas in complex, nautilus-like chambers. It could modify pressure across its many membranes to determine its altitude. "Roo," it sang, like a sad pigeon, its song reverberating through Hugh's tiny heart.

He looked to the generous measure of whisky resting on the windowsill and followed his sudden urge to paw it to the floor. Draughts blew up between his rickety floorboards, the coolness keeping him awake. The evening's incident had him determined to think of something. Anything that would exact a change.

"Come to bed, honey."

It was his wife, Galoria. She stood on the threshold of their bedroom door, her claws stuck in the bedsheet that she held over herself. "Because I know you did enough to earn your keep today, right?"

Hugh looked at his phone. He had a ton of notifications on Super, all from other superheroes he'd seen that night. They proclaimed to be his friend and asked for a positive rating since Hugh was *a witness to my performance, bro, know what I'm saying? Poz-rate me and I'll poz-rate you back. We're all in this together, buddy!*

He had only one new freely volunteered review. From Bobbie, the victim. It was far from glowing.

Hugh quoted the message to Galoria. "In *what* together?" he added. "I'm trying to do my job and they're all just getting in the way. It's just ridiculous that they trade these requests with me like we're buddies. Think of all the successes I've had and the paltry efforts these people make. It's not tough in the slightest to find someone who'll say something nice about your work."

"Can we not?" Galoria said. "You're doing fine, okay?"

"All the saves I've made. All these years gone by. Still, no one's ever, *ever* requested me by name."

She gave him a look.

He held his paws up. "I know, I know. I'm not even allowed to complain."

"Just come to bed."

"I can't sleep."

"Well, don't just stay up drinking," she said. "There are plenty of people out there needing rescued."

Hugh looked at the map on his phone. Sure enough, there were many people in his area. "But they're just a bunch of level ones. I don't even know how people get themselves in these easily escapable situations."

She crossed her paws. "Well, *I* was raised to believe no job was beneath me."

"So you admit what you're doing is beneath you? That is, 'No job'?"

She let out a low growl. "If you think vigilante justice is a difficult market to crack, how great a time of it do you imagine us cops are having? I don't care if they're flybots, ubercrabs, cyberparrots with learned helplessness or nihilistic owls. You better get out there and be the best damn vanquisher of level ones the city's ever seen because you have a damn mortgage to pay!"

With that, she slammed the bedroom door shut.

Hugh went to the bathroom to take off his costume. He unpinned his cape and hung it up in the shower to dry. With a sharpened claw, he tore a line down the back of the spandex and stepped out of it.

Once dressed in a pair of boxers and a satin smoking jacket, he returned to the living room-slash-kitchen, pouring himself another measure of whisky.

The most recent remake of his life story played on the TV. He reclined in front of it on a pile of clean clothes. One scene insinuated he'd had more than a bromance with The Big Nip, which became as good as reality as far as the city's humans were concerned. They made crude remarks about wanting to try out a cat's barbed member when he passed them in supermarkets and wine shops.

He scoffed. "What do I even matter?" He fell asleep as entire planets digitally crumbled on the screen before him.

Pete and Geoff hopped off the roof of the Z train onto a drainpipe that passed by their flat.

They padded over to the window of their human flatmate, Geronimo, and pawed at the glass, meowing.

Geronimo spent a good fifteen minutes trying to ignore them. They watched, thinking he hadn't heard them. He had to move to scratch his balls, and then they knew he was awake, so they meowed harder. Soon he was up.

He opened the window, fixing his tousled hair. "This is the last time you do this."

"Sure," Pete said.

"We just had to rush out and didn't have time to grab our keys," Geoff said.

They knocked some photos of Geronimo's girlfriend to the ground as they hopped onto his nightstand and traversed his bed, wandering down the corridor.

"Wait!" Geoff said as Pete stuck his head in their bedroom. "Don't you wanna stay up and play something with me?"

Pete yawned but whispered back, "Sure."

"W-We don't have to if you don't feel like it. If you want to be alone or whatever."

"No, let's," Pete said.

They scampered into the living room and to opposite ends of Geronimo's couch, scratching the corners. But their claws slid off. It was smooth.

"Hey!" Pete went to flick on the lights, then looked back at the couch.

"Unfair!" Geoff said.

Geronimo had taped scratching pads to its sides.

"Well, that's put me out the mood," Pete said.

Geoff had packed their side of the living room with all manner of colourful supermammal-themed posters, figurines, plushes, stacks of videogames, Blu-rays and card games. He used a special hovering shelf set that Pete got him for Cat Kwanza to display his most prized possessions, gifts from fellow supermammals and vanquished villains. A worn-out electric stinger from The Wasped Bastard. The singing pelt of Bison Conan. The shell helmet of Argonaut Francesco.

They heard now the springs, like Slinkys, of their electric pets, that came to greet them with glee. Pete stroked one now as he and Geoff scanned their possessions, Geoff with a look of pride, Pete with repressed bitterness.

Geoff hopped onto the couch and looked at his laptop on the coffee table, nudging it open with his nose. "Oh God," he said.

"What?"

"The humans have made another incest porn parody of us."

"They really won't give that name a rest, will they?"

Pete had once been half of the dynamic duo known as The Lavender Brothers. When that didn't work out, he placed an ad online looking for a new sidekick, worried that he was spending too much time alone in general. He picked Geoff because he was attracted to him. Pete still had the rights to The Lavender Brothers, so he continued to use the name, but once he and Geoff started officially dating, they had to change the name. As far as porn was concerned, however, the name was set.

"You wanna watch it?" Geoff said. He'd clicked the play button. Human men, wearing rubber cat masks, went at it. As a manx, Geoff had only a stump where a tail was in other cats. The stump wagged suggestively. He'd had strange-looking metal couplings drilled into it so he could attach weaponry.

Pete pawed the laptop shut. "Every human porn actor in this city is a failed superhero. It's just too sad to watch them."

"What then? You wanna watch the special edition of Truck Driver: Origins with me?"

"Not that one."

"Oh! I just got the boxset of Diarrhea Boy's first cartoon. Twenty-fifth-anniversary edition!"

"Those play on TV all the time, love."

"There's a new trailer for AnthropomorPhil's remake! I signed up early to watch it, so we get a bonus five seconds! We have to watch it, right now! Please?"

"Tomorrow, maybe."

"Oh! You wanna play a game, then? I just got The Great Shoeboxer version of Monopoly if you want? I promise not to get mad at you when I lose. You're just really good at it!"

Pete sighed. "Thank you, love. But after tonight, I don't think I can handle any supermammal stuff. I'm gonna stay on call. You don't have to come with me."

Geoff looked dejected. He tried to hide it by licking his paws, which Pete lamented. Geoff was too astute not to notice how much he irritated Pete with his neediness. "Ever since we met," he said, "we've always rescued together."

"But you don't want to."

"But we've never not done it together!"

Pete kicked away an itch in his neck. "Yeah, but maybe that's not a good thing."

"I guess," Geoff said.

Pete looked at Super on his phone. Truth was, Geoff had dragged them both way down in the rankings. Their map was almost completely empty. There was some extremely low-level work so far away that by the time they'd flown there, the attack would be over. Someone else was sure to snap them all up. He surreptitiously flicked to reveal the listings on ToxoplasmosList.

He grinned. "We're getting a call already!"

"Really?" Geoff shuffled into a comfy corner. "You're gonna be okay by yourself, right?"

How could Pete reassure his partner without sounding like it was no loss to rescue without him? He simply nodded and went to collect his keys by the door.

"Pete?" Geoff said, just as Pete was leaving.

"Uhuh?"

"I don't wanna be a supermammal anymore."

Pete purred compassionately and left.

"Unbelievable."

Katya, Ms T.N.T. herself, sat on the office desk in the corner of her husband's study, in his family's Edwardian manse. She was watching vloggers comment on her latest rescues. These took precedence over the many blog posts and social media feeds she had open, written by more successful supermammals who gave seminars and tips about the various minutiae of the job: "Top Ten Ways to Land"; "The Best Supermammals of the Twentieth Century"; "My Favorite Supermammals Reveal the Contents of Their Utility Belts"; "How to Recover from

Arch Nemesis Defeat." They were always positive, always encouraging, and never questioned whether there was a need for as many supermammals as there were. Katya thought every supermammal, aspiring or otherwise, would feel just that little less lonely if others admitted these vacillations. But maybe other supermammals thought that if they weren't seen to encourage others into the profession, they'd be seen as bitter and hypocritical, and no one would request them for rescues anymore. Or maybe they were in denial, more afraid of market saturation than the return of Doctor Insanophile.

"Noise, all of it!"

The inboxes of Katya's social media accounts flooded with the penises of humans, cats and indistinguishables of all variety. She got hundreds of crude comments about what various animals wanted to do to her if she'd let them. She soon deleted everything, but there were still dedicated fan pages on all the most popular sites. These mainly featured male humans dressing up as cats and ejaculating onto figurines of her. They'd take photos of the aftermath and share them with others, who enthusiastically complimented their efforts.

"Ms TNT is BOMBING!" said ElephantGazebo. She was one of the more popular blue-dreadlocked, manga-cat-t-shirt-collecting bipolar vloggers with a septum piercing. Though there was one like her *without* the septum piercing, called FoxFacedStaple, who had five subscribers more.

"This evening's latest attempted slime rescue was her worst blunder yet," ElephantGazebo continued. "All primed to go out with a bang. She had her prize pulled out from beneath her whiskers by The Lavender Pusses. Plus? Her outfits are looking sluttier than ever. The leather boots, the red bikini over the white leotard, and the cape that gets shorter every year! Here she is today, and here's what she looked like yesterday."

"Everything okay, lovey?" In strolled St John St John, her husband. He wore a pinstripe suit and held a leatherbound cat pocket-sized volume of Hegel under one arm. "You haven't sunk into the echo chamber again, have you?" He pouted, then drawled, "They're all having too much fun to notice their insignificance. I pity anyone who could be jealous of *that*."

"What can I say?" she said. "After a night like tonight, I'm just pleased to hear them talking about me."

She looked around the office. It was packed with travel guides, astrophysics non-fiction and enormous coffee table books on architecture, advertising, photography and the history of ghosts. Her barbed tongue licked at her lips in thought. She missed hanging out with Geoff. He'd turned his flat into a shrine to all things supermammal. Meanwhile, she had to creep into this office late at night if she wanted to watch anything supermammal-related, and was ashamed to talk of her "trivial profession" with St John.

"I'm proud of you no matter what, dear." He kissed her on the forehead.

"Then why be proud at all?"

She couldn't help her instincts. She batted him several times about the face in response then ran out of the room. Before she could re-enter and lick herself to pretend nothing had happened, she heard him locking the door.

"Oh, man." She padded up the stairs of the manse, passing portraits of her husband and his predecessors in soldier's garb. Berets, helmets and Queen's guard hats. Strings of heavy medals painted so meticulously they seemed to shimmer beneath the sooty light— human male strippers lined the balustrades, holding candles in outstretched arms.

She stopped on the landing to claw at the carpet directly above St John's office, knowing he would feel the vibrations.

In their bedroom, she decided to climb the velvet curtains to cheer herself up, but ended up stuck on the brass railing.

She meowed for one of the strippers to come and get her.

An oiled-up Greek dude in a spangly gold Speedo came in and stood by the curtains.

Once upon his shoulders, she misjudged a leap towards the bed, managing to get her claws in a silk sheet, only to slide it to the floor and over her head.

She ran back around the room in a circle, trying to get out, eventually skittering beneath the bed, having given herself a scare. St John would have loved to see her doing that. He supported her with the endless supply of money inherited from his legendary family, providing his feline lover with money as a dealer might distribute his catnip, to keep her sated and quell her complaints.

Katya looked at the cat's face repeated in the carpet pattern beneath her claws. St John's grandfather, may he rest in peace. "Why live this life that's been lived and will be lived over and over and over?"

"Because it's your turn, miss," the stripper said, looking at her beneath the bed.

"Is that all there is to it?"

"Mhm. Now, aren't you having fun?"

"Are you?"

"Sadness is not in my job description, ma'am."

She wept. How was she to define herself in the post-supermammal era? She had a great figure for her age but had outgrown the trophy wife shtick, could no longer think of being a supermammal as a silly little pursuit in which her husband's money allowed her to dabble. It was crushing to do it this long and be so far from the top.

She took out her phone. It made a sinister glowing blue mask of her furry face. She dialled Hugh.

He picked up. "Y-Yeah?"

"Wanna meet for a drink?"

CHAPTER THREE

"What brings us here?" Hugh's seductive hooded eyes filled with misery.

He met Katya at a seedy bar nearby, where the palm tree wallpaper was nicotine-stained, the tables looked like they were melting and the other animal patrons were obviously diseased.

"Hopefully you're not going to tell me to pick myself up and get back in the game," Katya demurred. "My own life's a mess. How the hell am I supposed to keep helping others?"

The gecko bartender handed Katya a catnip spliff. She lit and duly puffed on it before handing it to Hugh.

"Anyway," she continued, "I think we can solve the supermammal crisis, if you're interested."

Hugh sniffed, passing his martini from paw to paw. "That's nice, but it's not what brings us here."

"What are you talking about?"

"Ms TNT—"

"Katya, please."

"It's three a.m. You invited me out for a drink beside a motel that provides rooms by the hour?"

"Oh, come on!" She had another toke.

Hugh took it from her and had a puff. "So, Katya, you're going to deny it? You rush out here in what I assume is one of your husband's overcoats, and you're still wearing the boots of your costume. You'd risk losing anonymity just to turn me on?"

"As if it matters anymore," she said. "Even if I was exposed—"

"Hmmm."

"—there aren't even any villains left to avenge themselves. That's what I wanted to talk about."

"Don't talk." He pounced on the bar and bit her scruff. "Only fuck."

"Oh!" She scratched off her coat and joined him on the bar, presenting herself, her pussy pussy dripping with excitement.

Most of the animal patrons cheered. Some threw boots, only because the noise was distracting. Hugh's barbed pecker was soon inside her. How did hormones always have her forgetting how painful sex was for cats?

"How do you make a hormone?" Hugh said. "Be a cat and fuck her!"

His dick punched inside her and dug itself into her insides as he attempted to thrust. Now she was pissed off and wailing, but he bit her scruff harder. Minutes later, he was done.

She was raw and just as frustrated as before.

"I'm ready to go again," he said.

"You'd better be," she said, "because that was shit."

"A case of catnip dick. It'll pass."

"Get us a room this time. We'll wreck the minibar and I'll tell you my idea."

Pete stalked the streets.

How had he ended up here, amidst these ugly brutalist towers of concrete? They were first erected when the city was under communist rule, since awkwardly disguised by slugs that ran their lume-filled slime over the buildings, so they glowed in the dark. Their organic paint was the only source of light for Pete's walk.

He paced dreamily between splashes of neon, wondering why he'd never achieved the fame and fortune of his more successful rivals—like The Angry Dander, say, or Jeff. Or any of them who smiled at conventions and said stuff like, "Don't do this just so you can smile at convention audiences!"

Pete seethed as he remembered how they had feigned bemusement at their own success. How they had patronized him by saying that the work was its own goal. They hadn't realized that his envy of them had eclipsed the work's inherent joy, the joy that had gotten him started in the first place.

What a cop-out, Pete thought. Surely they just didn't want the competition, were thinking only of themselves, of the unlikelihood that there was room for him at the top tier alongside them.

Homeless catfish, begging saltopuses and gypsy squirrels passed him by, as he thought they might. He'd taken this route hoping their misfortune would cat-alyze a fountainhead of newly discovered gratitude in him; instead, his growing frustration refused to dissipate and the gnawing emptiness of his soul amplified.

"Rreow?" Pete arrived at the entrance of a car park, lit in chemical light. He looked at the address on his phone. Sure enough, he was directly in front of the—

KaPOW!

Something burst through the wall behind him. Chips of cinderblock whipped at him as they flew by, almost pinning him in a wreck of rubble. Scrambling to get on his back, he saw a lava pus tank. It glowed red and yellow, dripping obscenely like an infected cake. The ground beneath it flooded with a clear stream of fish guts and plankton, purplish and viscid.

Maniacal laughter erupted from the top of the tank, where three punk-looking men emerged, holding what looked like rocket launchers over their shoulders.

"Got ourselves a puss!" the main one said, standing atop the tank's turret.

"Oh my! It's one of those sexy Lavender ones," another man said, his mortar shell-encrusted helmet peeking over the turret's rim.

The tank careened forwards.

Pete hacked up mortar dust and brick bits. He cleaned himself from the mess of material around him and got on his feet, scampering into the car park. He heard the tank behind him, and a *crash* as it dinked the roof of the park on its way in. Purple fluid lapped at Pete's hind feet behind him as he scampered ahead. Caroming round a corner, he headed down a slope to the floor below. The tank was in close pursuit.

Floom. Rocket launcher devices fired spider webs that splatted on the walls on his way down—they were trying to catch him! And then? Oh, well, he just had to stop that from happening!

Running a decent distance from the tank, he turned to look at it and whipped out his sonic meow blaster.

The tank's tracks mashed cars to the floor. Waves of red lightning propagated across everything they touched.

"MEOWWW!" Pete screamed into his little plastic blaster.

Visible *MEOW!*s flew out. They were in bold-coloured letters, on bursts of contrastingly coloured spiked speech bubbles. They tore through the concrete of pillars and roofs on their approach. The men tried to dodge, but a stray *MEOW!* caught the guy whose head stuck out the hatch. The *M* of it lodged deeply into his head, splitting it in two. His green blood pumped out at an alarming rate, big thick ropes of it solidifying and yelling for help. His own scream came out weird, a fully functional brain no longer controlling his voice. The tank swerved left into a row of lady motorbikes, which streamed like wells of tears into a collective pool of melted metal.

Floom. More spider webs. They'd designed this encounter to trap Pete in the car park, which surely led underground, to a dead end. He didn't have many more tools at his disposal to take out the other two men. One of them now climbed down the tank in asbestos boots and crouch-walked in front of the tank, steadying his aim.

Wait! Pete scampered one floor more below and removed a bag of a special compound Geronimo had created for him in his meth lab. He sliced the bag open, careful not to touch the yellow crystals inside. In simply meeting the air, they fizzed. He felt the heat of them eat through the bag, which he couldn't hold onto for long.

Here came the tank again. Finger-like projections of fish guts crawled ahead of it.

Pete took aim and flung the bag. It landed in the fluid, which simmered ferociously. The thick puddle turned black, bubbles popping from its surface and emitting a screaming smoke. The remaining man on the tank's turret made to dive off, suspecting what was about to happen. But it was too late. The guts ate a hole out the floor, the tank and the man fell through. *Crash crash crash*. The momentum sent it through many more floors below.

"Oh, you're gonna get it, pussy!" the last man said.

"Reow!" Pete meowed angrily. All he had to do was get beyond this one guy and scamper back out of the car park to safety. He leapt onto one car, another, flipping like a starfish through the air high above the last man.

Floom.

A web ate Pete up. Streams of the net's silk squirmed against him, and his balled-up body fell through the hole left by the tank. He scrambled to turn the right way, limbs emerging through inopportune gaps in the web, but as he disappeared through the hole to the sound of a mournful meow, his legs stuck out at such an angle that he would surely land with great pain.

"Sexy lil" puss," the punk said, rubbing the thigh leather of his chaps. He stalked towards Pete, who sat on the cooled, hardened lava pus at the tip of the tank's wreckage. The tank's back half had collapsed on impact. The upper half jutted upwards towards the hole through which it had fallen.

Pete looked behind him. A shaft of strip-light came from the hole above and illuminated a beautiful splash of orange that fanned out in all directions from the shattered skull of the fallen punk. Little balls of brain tumbled down the mounds of broken concrete. Their thoughts of abusive childhoods, weird extreme sex and illicit substances expired with each *boing* of a bounce.

Pete was on his back, limbs held askew by the bag of web. The spiders of it weaved tighter and tighter, leaving his genitals exposed.

"I wanna suck on that barbed lil' dick, boy!" The last punk crawled towards Pete. His erection plinged off the tank's wheels as he climbed up one of the tracks. He soon hunched over Pete's little body.

A familiar whirring sound reverberated around the room, followed by an angry "Reow!"

"Ahh!" The punk screamed and looked down at Pete for pity—but he found only shock in the furry little expression that looked back at him. The punk grit his teeth hard. Blood flowed over his gums. Lava lamp-like drips of blood and saliva dropped onto Pete's costume.

The punk collapsed to reveal Geoff, withdrawing his conical drill tip tail extension from the punk's rectum. He un-clicked the extension from the coupling he'd had drilled into his manx stump. The shock of the drilling sound had sent him into one of his default cat modes. Distracted, ignoring Pete, he licked the drill tip clean of gore.

"Geoff!"

"Reow? Oh, Pete! You're okay!"

Geoff scratched the net open and the two embraced.

"You left ToxoplasmosList open for me to find, didn't you?" Geoff said. "Were you trying to hurt me? Were you so desperate to get rid of me? And you must think I'm so difficult to talk to that you'd rather put yourself in danger."

"I'm so sorry, my love. You're right. I was dishonest. I betrayed your trust."

Geoff licked at Pete's ear fur "I'm just glad you're safe."

"Friends," Hugh said, taking a swig of Herr Krapper's Twig and Berry Wine from a flask-shaped bottle in his kilt. He vomited. "Bleuuurgh! Too much liquid courage. Sorry, friends. I'm nervous."

"Thank you for coming here tonight," Katya said, addressing the roomful of supermammals of every rank. She ushered Hugh behind the blue flow of glowing sewage from a grated pipe above, which caught irradiated fish heads, talking bones and other associated organic trash. It was the runoff of a luxury litter factory that ran twenty-four hours for four months without stopping, creating the finest, desiccated particles from pulverized bones of animals with a lineage.

Supermammals grimaced in confusion, mewled with disappointment and stuck up their rears. They were ready to pounce. Katya was responsible for calling them to the heart of the planet, to its liquid core of glowing sewer water? Why?

"We didn't mean to trick you," she continued. She'd made a fake post on Super to attract everyone. "I mean, was it a trick, really? All of you know there isn't a supervillain of the magnitude we posted about. There hasn't been one like our invention for far too long now. But you came here because you hoped there was."

"And that was exactly our meaning." Hugh flipped up his kilt to clear his face of vom.

"Huh," said The Gant Summer Line. It was just a bunch of posh sweaters, associating in a loose ball of crime-fighting wool, evidence that the definition of 'supermammal' was now as loose as the weave of its fabric. It looked up Hugh's kilt. "He hasn't been spayed."

"Yeah, well," said Benevolent Genius Intersex Person, "takes balls to do whatever this is."

"Let's not kid ourselves any longer," Katya said. "I know for many of you this is a passion. For some, it's a hobby that exploded into a profession. Whatever this is, there is or used to be a huge amount of pleasure or purpose gained from vanquishing villains. But never more in this city's history have there been so many heroes per villain."

"But not all is lost," Hugh said. "Tonight, we declare the first official meeting of the SMC Supervillain Alliance."

"What?" said I.D.S: The Irritating Dentistry Student. "You can't be serious. I would never be the conscious agent of anyone's misfortune."

"Don't you see that you already are?" Katya said. "The most benevolent thing you can hope to do is steal someone else's rescue mission. If you're lucky enough to feed your family in this line of work, it means depriving dozens, nay, hundreds of others from doing the same."

"I-It doesn't work like that."

"Oh, grow up!" Hugh, having hit the bottle so hard all evening, had reached that stage where it was tough to get any drunker than he was, and a hangover approached. "This isn't a fucking blog post we're talking about anymore. This is real. Right here. What we're proposing is serious. Lonely Sadist Internet Troll, right?"

"Uhuh."

"Don't be shy. Step forwards into the light and tell everyone your ranking."

The room gasped. Such a request was uncouth at best. Asking a lady her ranking was worse than asking her age—even if both figures were ultimately arbitrary.

"2493756."

"Memorised down to the last unit," Hugh said.

"Many a mammal has exploded overnight. It just takes that next opportunity."

Hugh tutted and waved away the end of her sentence. "Doesn't exist."

"Yes it does!" she protested. "Just last month, The Living Swine rescued The Lord of High Kittydom's third cousin twice removed from a megabeak bludgeoning in the Savage Quarter. It's not just the size of the rescue but the reputation of the victim." At that, she folded her forefeet and simpered.

"Hah! Sorry. There's something so funny about the word 'beak.'"

"If I may, Hugh?" Katya shot him a bitter look for getting everyone off track. "Don't you agree that there isn't just the rescue in this equation, but the creation of the rescue opportunity that makes a great hero? That we can expand the operations of supermammals by increasing the net total woe? That there is, if I may say so, a necessary evil required?"

"I-I suppose," Troll said.

Little leathery pads clapped together at this contribution.

"Then let's be that necessary evil," Hugh said. "Let's create opportunities for heroes by being villains! Think back to your childhood, running around your garden with a figurine of

Fridge Boy or Bruce, Head of Marketing, imagining all kinds of dangers they got themselves into. Together we have the power, creativity and experience to create a villain more epic than the city's ever seen! They want villainy? Well, let's give it to them! They want fame and recognition? Let's make them earn it! With our combined evil, no longer will we have to learn about every insipid little squib who ever fucked over a fellow supermammal to save a bingorat! What do you say?"

Many supermammals had already flown away. Some who remained tried to dial the police—but then several brutal-looking pusses stepped forwards from the darkness into the sickly light of the streaming sewage. They batted away the do-gooders' mobiles, glaring at them until they too fled.

Katya smiled at those who stayed. "You may all now consider yourselves members of The SMC Supervillain Alliance."

It was morning, and Geronimo was cooking meth. A pungent gas, the scent of nosebleeds, emanated from his lab at the flat's rear.

Pete and Geoff scratched at the door. For the privilege of subletting in the Pusses' flat, Geronimo had to put up with their sporadic whining. Sometimes for chemical weapons. Other times, like now, they wanted food and affection.

Geronimo left his lab, wearing only a pair of holed boxers, and sleepily stumbled into the kitchen. He took out bowls for the couple, launched dry food from a bag in the vague direction of both bowls, then stumbled back to his room.

"Dry food?" Pete said.

"Geronimo's having a tough time of it," Geoff said. "He's on a tight schedule."

They coyly pawed dry nuggets of the stuff back and forth to each other, a conversation soon developing.

"After we got married," Geoff said, "I said I'd happily keep a home for us, raise a litter for us both. It's something we'd always talked about doing. You insisted we forgo that to remain supermammals together. You said it with such conviction that I never thought to question it."

Pete cracked a nugget with his incisors. "I didn't stop to think. It's just that, after marriage, kids were the next goal, and then that was it. That interesting life, which had seemed to stretch years ahead of us before, collapsed. We were at the finish line already. Our lives would be over, and I was scared they'd be for nought."

Geoff hesitated. He seemed careful to achieve the right tone. "You think you need to do more than enjoy yourself with me and a family to have your life mean something?"

Pete sighed. "Would you judge me if I said 'Yes'? Honestly, I don't know the difference between what I want and what I need. All the supermammals that made it tell you, 'Don't wait until you achieve this level of success to learn that it's not what's important in life.'" He wept now. "There are times we've been here at home and I've neglected to have fun with you because my mind's been on our Super ranking. It's just a game is all it is, and—my God—I was prepared to die for it!"

Geoff came closer and pawed the air in front of Pete's face as if practising the comforting stroke he was about to give.

"I recall now the words of Chekhov," Pete said. "'It is only a narrow-minded or embittered man who can harbour evil thoughts about ordinary people because they are not heroes.'"

"Hey," Geoff said. "You're the least narrow-minded puss I know. I love your mind so much. Hey. You are enough."

"Tonight was a wake-up call," Pete said. "I want you to know that. You matter more to me than this business. So let's find safer jobs."

"Get off my husband, you slutty little tomcat!" Galoria said. She slammed back the door to her husband's motel room. Hugh and Katya lay there on the bed, naked.

"Oh my!" Katya held up the sheet to hide her teats.

"Bitch." Galoria held her weapon steady. "Your husband knows, by the way. He called me up and paid me to come down here. He had his suspicions about you two."

"Galoria, please." Hugh got out the bed. "There's nothing between us. I'm doing this for you."

At this, Galoria pressed her paws to her head, reeling at the thought of it. She gestured to Katya with the pistol. "Doing *this*, for *me*?"

Hugh tried to suppress a purr. "We can talk about it when we get back home."

"No." Galoria's tears rolled over her fur. They magnified the glints of so many tortoiseshell colours. "You don't live with me anymore."

"Give him a chance to explain!" Katya ran to grab Galoria's forefoot as she made for the entrance again.

"Rreow!" Galoria snarled.

She spun around and—*bang*—shot Katya in the heart.

"Oh my Cat God." Galoria pressed a paw to her mouth, smearing her lipstick. She turned to Hugh. "Look at what you made me do."

"Get out!" His tail swished around, indicating an imminent clawing.

Galoria scampered away, leaving the door ajar, dropping the pistol on her way out.

Hugh ran to Katya and lapped at the blood that poured out of her. He licked the back of his paw and tried to rub it over the hole, as if that would do any good.

"I-It's okay." Katya stroked his side with her remaining might.

"How in the world is this okay?" His third eyelids crept in. He winced. Life ebbed away from his former lover.

"Now... you have... a tragic... backstory. Ahh."

"But I already had one of those," he said. "Doesn't that count for anything?"

With a final sigh, she was gone. But her spirit didn't travel far. It floated through the air and imbued Hugh with the purpose and conviction he needed to take their plan to its dreadful conclusion.

CHAPTER FOUR

Pete and Geoff set themselves to the task of casting off their former identities. Together, they acknowledged the large unlikelihood that their supermammal dreams would ever be realized. They knew now that the work of their spiritual ancestors in the field of supermammal justice, which had so inspired them, was representative of an inexplicable boom in villainy. The victories of that era were the biggest the industry would ever see. And so they sat with laptops on their bellies, on Geronimo's scratched-up couch, looking for new jobs.

Pete accepted a position at a post office in the hate mail department, where he would sort bombs, threats, angry words, sickly ink, acids, anthrax, dead animals and excrement. Sometimes even razor blades—often coated with dangerous infectious diseases—glued into pieces of paper which, when torn apart, would slice the fingers of the recipient's hands.

Pete marvelled, sadly, at the wealth of bizarre positions available within their little locus of planets in this corner of the universe. He trudged over to bookshelves in the living room and thumbed through a well-worn book on economic theory. Out loud, he read a solemn passage about the negative spiritual impact of division of labour.

This did nothing to comfort Geoff, who had just accepted a position at a factory that manufactured circuit boards used to detect the right time for lovers to spring out of birthday cakes. "I'm kinda relieved, though. I don't have to try at being a supermammal anymore. I don't think I ever was one."

Pete stroked his husband's tufty ears with pride.

Geoff held up his laptop to show Pete the location of his office: about five planets left of Pete's new job. "A long commute. We won't get to see each other so much."

Pete licked his paw and rubbed it on Geoff's head. "Then it will be all the sweeter when we do."

"The supervillains our city wanted," said a ginger reporter puss on the news. "Disgruntled ex-supermammals have formed a villainous alliance as a weird and counterintuitive response to the oversaturated supermammal market. Diana Catfish is reporting live from SMC Shore's military base, with this."

They cut to Diana, a slim black cat in a dark trench coat. "Thank you, Connie," said Diana, through wet and whiskered lips.

Rain, as if flung at her from buckets off-camera, coated the image on the screen. Viscous sighing mouths yawned without sound on their descent.

"Yes," Diana continued, "Hugh McElhatton, aka The Wee Jakey, is said to be the mastermind behind the surge in villainous acts over the last week. In letters to local newspapers, he said he's challenging the city to come up with a benevolent force big enough to counteract the evil he and his contemporaries plan to bring about. He's been ramping up these challenges week after week to the despondent and slovenly response of what is now a dearth of remaining supermammals, most of whom have been out of work for years. Sources tell us this challenge's penultimate act is occurring here and now, by this very military base."

Way out in the ocean, octonukes packed themselves into the seabed's seams, pushing their cephalic loads against one another and glowing resolutely.

A team of cat scientists observed this from the local military base. Kitties in lab coats gathered in a heavily armoured control room, which looked out upon the steely sea. They crowded around screens, noting observations. On their Geiger maps, the 'nukes looked collectively like two glowing angry eyes compressed in bulging, tapered lids of granite.

Hugh stood atop SMC Cathedral, wielding a loudspeaker and leaning off an ornate and pearly cross. He held the loudspeaker to his mouth and shouted, "Go!"

Waves of his words, in colourful speech bubbles, travelled towards the sea like *go-Go-go-Go*, echoing across the land and sky.

The kitties in the military base braced themselves as Hugh's *Go* reached them. Rolling *GO!* bubbles spun out in streams across the sea, moving with enough speed to stay on the water's surface until they were within sufficient range of the 'nukes.

A Siamese general watched this with horror. "Oh no!"

Like big cookies decorated in colorful icing, the bubbles dropped over the horizon. Seconds later, a low and foreboding *boom* sounded out.

Kitties crowded around a live map of the seabed—but it crackled and went out of focus.

"Come on!" said one of the controllers.

She pawed at the monitor to refocus the image. When it came back, the glowing octonuke eyes had exploded, creating tsunami waves, big uncontrollable walls of nuke-steeped water taking over the sky.

The tsunami thundered off the sea and across the land. It obliterated the enormous crumbling-yet-proud buildings, which had defined the old town, with the ease of a giant's somnambulant stomp, seawater pouring through the city.

A colourful army of artists—cartoonists, dancers, musicians, comedians and more— stood proudly on the streets. Low energy streams of the dying tsunami flushed around their legs.

Before them were a different group of soldiers, who were all in black riot gear, their many heads swarming like the angry, shiny knuckles of mashed, demonic hands. Their clear shields had Hugh's face on them, spray-painted there by hand.

The rival groups shouted at one another.

A young man with technicolour hair spoke on the TV. He was clearly from the artist's crowd. "There has never been a better time for us," he said. "The city needs to heal. We're out here on the frontline giving the people what they need!"

The soldiers in black riot gear threw nail bombs at undeserving civilians. Nails tore through flesh with ease, creating grim pincushions of bodies and faces.

A group of ballet dancers stood close, improvising a dance to the sound of cracking bones. Upon witnessing the majesty of their dance, the injured humans rejected the nails from their bodies and recuperated in mere moments.

Sketch artists sat on the frontline by canvases. Just as Monet had once attempted to capture the motion of light on water, so did they sketch the path of flying bullets with such astute observation and grace that when those same bullets became embedded in their flesh, they were already immune to the damage.

Impersonators satirized the soldiers' stances, to the hilarity of innocent bystanders. This had the soldiers falling to their knees in response to the vicious effect of ironic humour.

Short story writers were out there, kneeling in the water. They had wry smiles on their twisted faces and laptops open on their pyjama shorts. They positively lampooned their enemies. The stories themselves, emailed around mere minutes later, proceeded to do untold damage, thousands of words painting pictures so tragic that the soldiers lost their minds.

These acts of art were merciless. But the villains weren't done yet.

A fleet of modified carrier jets dropped bombs, each the strength of a dozen poems. The artists couldn't keep up, yielding to the blast, souls relinquishing their bodies to their inescapable, pulped fate.

"This is a call to all remaining supermammals!" Diana Catfish was back on the TV again. She and the cameraman floated around on satellite dishes that they'd tied together into a raft. "This is a job big enough for all of you. We will not survive without everyone's participation."

Pete and Geoff watched the TV in their apartment. A wave took over the screen, the water pushing up against the glass of it. The TV soon burst, the flood pouring into Pete and Geoff's living room and soaking their carpet.

Geronimo came out of his lab, followed by weird orange vapours that billowed around the ceiling. He looked at the mess and stamped his feet. "Aw, man! Living with you cats is too much."

"It's okay, Geronimo," Pete said. "Geoff and I are going to fix this."

"The water damage?"

"No, the city, duh!" Geoff tutted. A kipper had swum into the living room and he'd caught it in his mouth

"I don't care about the city!"

"Okay," Pete said, "but if we promise to fix the water damage, will you help us?"

"You guys are my landlords. You're contractually obliged to—okay, fine! Come into my lab and I'll show you my latest chemical weapons. Reds turn you inside out, greens cause financial crises, blues are known to contribute to suicidal thoughts in mice—hey!"

Pete and Geoff skittered quickly into the lab and nabbed bags of oranges, purples and yellows, then they scampered out the apartment.

"My fellow enemies!" Hugh stood atop the dome of the city's cathedral. He swung from its cross, which was made from scallop shells and assorted beach knick-knacks. The cathedral proper was coated in layers of artificially coloured sand, like one of those displays in a bottle.

He swigged from a big white bottle of bleach. Big stars, which looked like they were made of dripping plastic, took over his vision. The villain alliance below became a heart-shaped blur of finger puppet beasts in colourful outfits.

"Phase One is complete!" he said. "If that didn't get their attention, we're all fucked. Are you ready to see what this city's made of?"

"Yeah, why not?" they cried back. "We weren't really doing anything else."

"Cool. Enemies assemble! They approach."

A flock of supermammals appeared down a clear path, which led from the sea all the way up to the cathedral's square. They darted towards the cathedral, between the girders, brick piles and other detritus.

Fountains of vomit shot out at them from the windows of adjacent buildings. Hugh had channelled these using his fully formed powers. He pressed his paws to his temples, psychically sending out pulses of melting sinks, couches, chairs, beds, windows, toilets and associated domestic ephemera from nearby windows on the supermammals' path.

Highlight-She, Countess of Office Supplies, had turned herself over to villainy. She used her powers to command standing desks, pairs of monitors, rolls of tape, sticky notes, coffee machines and conical cups into a deadly stream that she flung in a zigzag pattern between the buildings. This administrative effluvium smashed into the occasional supermoose or flying wombat.

Some heroes looked back on this sight with sorrow, but most gritted their teeth and kept flying ahead.

Geoff and Pete were at the very front of the supermammal formation. They dodged as Nitrogeena, Queen of the Air's Most Abundant Inert Gas, sent pockets of nitrogen directly into their faces, hoping to knock them out.

Landing about a block away from the cathedral, supermammals wrestled with Cable Lad's cables. They burst from the asphalt, whipping around, sparks flying in all directions. A wave of animals stayed to deal with this task while Pete and Geoff led the remaining crew forwards to deal with ExistentiaLisa. She stood in front of them, her panther legs stretched into a black leotard with "EL" embroidered on the front in silver lettering. She sobbed.

"Oh honey!" said Honeybear Hunnigan. "Are you okay?"

"Stay away from her!" said Catalina, The Extrovert that Sets Your Teeth on Edge. "She's up to no good."

Hunnigan stroked ExistentiaLisa's hair and filled with the horror, the horror. Both dropped to the fetal position and rocked back and forth as pulses of the meaninglessness of it all ran through them.

"We have to keep going!" Geoff looked ahead at the cathedral. Hugh's regurgitative attacks had cleansed it of sand brought in by the tsunami. It was now a white strip of bone between the surrounding greying masses of wet destruction.

"Look there!" Pete pointed to the grimy green costume of a rainforest frog stuck to the side of the crumbling business district. "It's the Embarrassing Fungoloid."

The Fungoloid belched. Weird, dark green particles flew out its mouth towards the crew. They tried to outrun it, but the particles caught Emotional Intelligence Champion and Excellent Personality Girl in their greasy network. Weird outcrops, like growths from the eyes of potatoes, coated the surfaces of their skin. They writhed in pain.

"Enough!" Pete stood at the foot of the cathedral now, picking up one of the loudspeakers Hugh had accidentally dropped from up above. "This ends here!" He was calling to the roof, but nothing appeared.

"Supervillains unite!" Hugh called down. So he *was* up there!

All manner of villains, hundreds of them, filtered past Pete and Geoff's team as they returned from the fight in the streets back to the cathedral.

Long slits opened at the cathedral's corners. In flooded all of Geoff's former favourites: The Black Fingernail; The Guy Who Painted All of History's Horse Portraits; The Cog: Half Cat, Half Dog; The Building Blocks of Life; E.G.E: Evidence that God Exists; Scarily Persistent Couch; Scandinavian Furniture Fucker and many others, all piled on top of each other in elevators embedded in the cathedral's columns.

Click.

Streams of dust formed a blanket around the rim of the cathedral. Its dome lifted to reveal the enormous limestone face of an angry cat skull, which rose up on a stalk.

The main cuboid of the cathedral tilted up and landed on one of its shorter sides. Its entrance now faced the ground. The skull lowered itself back down on the main structure, which was to be its body. Four columns—two towards the skull and two at the ground—winged out from the body. All four angled downwards. They were the cathedral's legs.

High above, Hugh hung from the limestone skull. "Behold!" He siccuped a little, then wiped the spittle from his chin. "Her name is Cat-Thedra!"

Cat-Thedra took off into the sky.

Pete and the others flew up towards Cat-Thedra. He circled the square, claws emerging from his columnar forefeet, big knives they were. He used them to score his way through shopping centres, historical spires and the houses of Parliament.

"How do we fight her?" Geoff stared in awe at Cat-Thedra's structure. He was twice as high as any building Geoff had ever seen.

"Keep flying up!" Pete and his hero crew followed Cat-Thedra into the upper atmosphere, blue sky giving way to black space, which swiped the heat from their little bodies.

Just before his body froze completely, Pete spun around to face the others, looking into all their petrified faces and reaching out a paw.

All their joints lost articulation. They yielded to the stasis of frost and drifted with what remained of their momentum. They agglomerated as if magnetically attracted to one another. Each was a jigsaw piece in a puzzle whose image remained unclear.

Until the final *click!*

Now, together they were a single, macroscopic super-superhero: The Iced Goodie. T.I.G.

The Ebony Gay Teen Dream Creampie Team made up most of her legs. They had sockets at their top. These fit neatly into the rounded divots of a torso made from Satyroman, The Human Eyebrow, Sclerodermina and Toilet Roll Absorbency Competitive with the Leading Brand Woman.

Forefeet extended from T.I.G.'s body. They were comprised of Birthweight Billy, Seafoam Sammy, Legs McGillicuddy and Foetal Alcohol Girl.

Creeping Life of Mediocrity Man was T.I.G.'s left fist, Unfulfilled Aspirations Boy its right.

At the helm, in a head composed of many more legendary heroes, were, of course, Pete and Geoff. Glassy lenses of ice kept them enclosed in the eyes, looking out.

Cat-Thedra followed, jets bursting from her charring lower legs, his skull rearing back, baring fangs.

Chomp. His jaws clamped down on T.I.G's leg, tearing the frozen bodies of several heroes off. He tossed his head and sent them floating out into space alone.

T.I.G screamed, her uvula of The Taxes Sisters reverberating with her cry.

Cat-Thedra carried onwards, holding out a forefoot, landing on the nearby planet of The Jigging Fox. He caved a square crater into the planet where his foot landed. The planet absorbed her shock and deviated from its orbit. Bouncing off and returning to T.I.G, the planet went careening into the pinkest of the system's three suns.

Cat-Thedra loaded villains into her arms. He stretched the arms out, firing Swedish Anxiety Girl, The Blasphemous Gurkha and Airhead Jimbob towards T.I.G. These mammalian bullets curled up, screaming silently as they froze.

T.I.G stretched out her arms. From her rear, the rocket powers of William Wallace and Sheep Paul fired up. This spun T.I.G. out of the bullets' range. She shed icy tears as the bullets, her former friends, disappeared into the epic darkness all around.

Time to go on the offensive! T.I.G swam through space towards a nearby dead plane. She broke off her tail of Polyamorous Polymer-Patty, Bobby the Brahmin and Hair Metal Mona. They curled up like a row of doughnuts and became the straw through which T.I.G sucked at the planet. She cracked its thin surface, imbibed its white-hot core. Her belly expanded tenfold, a stomach of superheroes distending into a thin, glowing net. T.I.G turned back to Cat-Thedra and discharged her full load of heat at him. Tear-like formations solidified in space's merciless cold, begetting an unholy ferrous rain.

Cat-Thedra yowled as the rain chipped at his bone. His face lost the fearsome look of tenacity it had achieved with its frowning eye sockets and sharp teeth. Every inch of his skull was now pitted into the shapeless mass of a lonely moon.

Cat-Thedra's roared, firing up the propulsion devices of his lower limbs. This sent him back towards T.I.G, feet flailing with a desperate attack of freeform karate. He slammed into T.I.G's chest and sent them both, a combined projectile, plummeting back to the surface of Supermammal City.

Pete and Geoff watched pitilessly through T.I.G's eyes as Cat-Thedra failed to withstand re-entry. Debris flew off left and right, his body stripping its protective white brick. This revealed the petrified innards of villains, which themselves sloughed off from the structure. Cat-Thedra lost its mass to become just cat, singular: Hugh, his matted fur flapping in the breeze of descent.

Pete and Geoff, looking to each other. They, too, had lost their armour. Each superhero of their super-superstructure was now just a reheated, individual unit, flailing in confusion through the air.

"Uff!"

Pete and Hugh slammed into the cavernous dent in the ground where the cathedral used to be. All that remained was crumbling dirt with bars of reinforcing steel poking out; multiple burst municipal pipes, which spewed fish guts meant for the punk district; seawater used as a coolant for the recently raided octonuke plant; and glowing sewage on its way to Hugh's first villain lair. All this swirled into a watery, greenish slime that formed a rising pool, with Pete on one side of it and Hugh on the other.

Up above, Geoff and the other beleaguered superheroes and villains gathered around the pit. All wanted to see what their leaders would do next.

Hugh staggered from paw to paw. "This is your fault, Pete!"

"*My* fault? You're delusional."

"No!" Hugh said. "Enough! I'm not going to listen to your self-serving narrative anymore. We were a team, brother. We were gonna be the best. And then, after one little fight, you abandoned me for Geoff!"

Pete looked up to Geoff, who ordinarily would have shied away from conflict; now, he observed the brothers with calm and compassion.

The villains booed Pete with their remaining energy. The irked heroes defended him with collectively incoherent shouts.

'that's right!" Hugh said. 'my brother fell in love and left me by the wayside. Then later, I cheated on my wife with Katya, and Katya died."

"Enough." Pete waved a dismissive paw. "You're still being a dick, bro."

"Also, my parents are dead."

"That's desperate, that is. Especially since we have the same parents, so it doesn't even count."

The heroes and villains had receded from the pit's rim. Most of them had fainted. Some of them even logged in help requests on Super, on both sides.

"I've gotta take you out, you understand," Pete said. "For my alleged betrayal, plus Katya's death, I'll give you a five-second head start. Then I'm coming after you."

Hugh's cape was notably tattered into a ghost-faced sheet. The mouth of it huffed out a sorry sigh. Pete stood for a moment, dreamily watching his brother take off, with contempt, before he gave chase. He scrambled out of the pit with Geoff's help. His husband also handed him all the crystal baggies of different colours, supplied by Geronimo. Pete was soon scampering through the square's battered battleground, holding the bags in front of him like some revered ceremonial torch.

Hugh ran through the surrounding apocalyptic streets, avoiding bursting manhole covers that curled up like tortillas and slammed back down into the asphalt. He downed the last of his bleach from a sealed plastic bag, followed by a pail of warm salt water and then held up a picture of a previous sick. This desperate tactic worked. Soon, as he hobbled ahead, he vomited into the wind, sending vaporous orange ghosts in Pete's direction. These caressed Pete's face, infecting him with self-doubt, fear, anger, anti-Semitism and itchiness. Pete clawed at his face, but kept running. Hugh, seeing this, ran up the eroded front of a bank. Arms, paws, hooves and claws burst out the bank's windows to hinder him.

Pete followed Hugh up the side of the building. He bit at the polythene wrapper of a bag of purple crystals, which floated out into the warm airstream blowing up the street. The crystals flowered into several wormy, barking sausages, which wiggled to maintain lift, singing their wormy song. They overtook Pete and spun now into helicopter blades, flinging themselves at Hugh's extremities. Slices chipped out Hugh's tail and lower legs. He grunted out, "Ugh," with each offence, but showed no sign of slowing down.

Hugh ran vertically now, up the building's Art Deco façade, dodging rhino horns and antelope necks and the assorted living obstacles that jutted out to stop him. Turning, he flung expanding, snapping turtle jaws over his shoulder.

To Pete, the turtle jaws looked like dead black pixels against the white sky's clarity. Soon they were tennis ball-sized disembodied snappers headed straight for Pete's face.

Pete shielded himself with his paws, the snappers clipping at him on their descent, taking little chunks from his belly and arms. One of the snappers got its grip between the bones of a forefoot. Pete grimaced but kept running, prying the snapper from himself and then pouring orange crystals into its maw. He then flung the snapper jaw back at Hugh and veered away from the resulting explosion.

Boom.

Hugh got coated with LSD-laced confetti.

Hugh was incapacitated by the time they reached the top of the building. He used all the might in his paws to drag himself onto the roof, where he lay wheezing.

Pete soon arrived at his side. "Enough, bro. I'm not going to have this end in the death of one of us. I have enough energy left in me to try and fix you just one last time. So why don't you tell me what this is about?"

Behind low white clouds that swooped around the rooftops were the vague black silhouettes of other combined beasts, much like T.I.G and Cat-Thedra. They had big barbed tongues, claws, hydraulic shovels and runaway tunnel boring machines with multiple villainous teeth. Together, they all ruined the city.

Hugh coughed out more paper. "Why does this have to be about anything at all?"

Superheroes and villains crawled to the top of the building to rejoin their leaders.

Pete tossed a topaz-coloured crystal at Hugh's face.

Geoff placed a paw on Pete's shoulder. The pair watched in awe as the crystal became an opaque yellow ball and landed *splat* on Hugh's nose. Googly eyes ebbed out its goo before it sucked itself up Hugh's nose. He gagged a bit, but soon passed out.

"That was amazing!" Geoff said.

Pete's tired little shoulders slumped forwards. "It was hardly the most purposeful thing I've ever done, defeating a villain who just fancied a scrap. But I guess someone had to do it."

"Not just someone," Geoff said. "*You* had to do it. Because he was your brother."

"Maybe. I wish you could've been by my side, though."

"No, you don't. I do, but you don't. This is something you were meant to do, but I never wanted to be a sidekick. I just wanted you and I got confused." He laughed bashfully.

"But I can't do this alone, remember?" Pete said. "I got in trouble so quickly."

They looked down at Hugh.

"Hey," Geoff said, "I know what everyone would love."

CHAPTER FIVE

"Hi! I'm Hugh McElhatton, formerly The Wee Jakey and brother of SMC's superhero-of-the-minute Pete, himself formerly half of The Lavender Pusses.

"You know, even before I was a villain, I had trouble finding meaning in life. If I wasn't putting myself in danger on the streets, I was at home, drinking too much and neglecting my wife. Some might say the good I did as a supermammal outweighs how I took her for granted. But I'd wager you don't know the pain of being the saviour of thousands but not of yourself, the hero in the eyes of a faceless mass but not in the eyes of your wife. I used to be a disgrace, and I've done some shameful things in my life, but I've repaid my debt to society. Now I spend my days concocting secret *benevolent* plans, thinking of new ways to help our city prosper. And *that's* what I wanted to talk to you about today.

"See, we need your unique talents for the new Supermammal Union, or S.M.U, formed in the wake of the wide-scale destruction that I wracked the city with a few years ago. It took artists a full *week* to repair the damage.

"Oh, what does it mean to be a cog in a rolling machine? To remain hopeful about life when you're doomed to die, to spill a drop of water into the ocean during a chronic, torrential storm and force a smile at this infinitesimal contribution? To climb on giants only to find unknown feet on your own shoulders the next day, talentless smarmers fitting you like a mammalian brick into the wall of progress *if you're lucky*? What's more likely is all your work will be for nought, you'll be forgotten, and you'll discover too late, if you discover at all, how you were supposed to have divided your meagre grains of time.

"Pete, listen, I won't be stifled. Just let me do me, and you can cut out the bits you don't like at the end, okay?

"Yes, everyone knows the top supermammals get all the prize kills, and they've worked hard for them and deserve them, *I* think. But villainy has many forms, many of them much smaller in scale and more pervasive. With the simple act of doing no harm, of promoting what you see as good in the world, all of us can work together to conquer evil. And that's what we at S.M.U think it takes to be a hero. It isn't all about the top. It's the accumulation of all of us combatting the minutiae of evil, day after day. It may not be glamorous, but there's always a need for every one of us, guaranteed! So let's be competitive no more. I don't know about you, but I've no control over the size of the part I play—so I decided recently just to be happy to have a part at all. Your part is there if you want it too. Just pick up the phone and give us a call. Registration takes only five minutes, and does...?"

"A World of Good!"

"That's right, thanks, gang!

"No matter what job you choose, you'll never know if you'd be happier or better put to use elsewhere. And sure, on our planet, there's a glut of other professions in a critical crisis. But—just be a supermammal anyway! I know you want to, and life is short, so fuck it! Fuck everyone!

"Pete, just keep quiet. It's almost over.

"We typically take a few working days to get back to you. In the meantime, please use your voice through your preferred medium to spread the word about us. Add to the billions of words, the scores of new music, the hours of footage, the lightyears of knitted material and what-have-you on the slightest chance you have something new to say to an undiscovered audience. Oh, I'm sorry, did you have a better plan?

"Pete, just do this last bit yourself. I can't help going off script. Take two?! No. Don't make me do this again. Just send me back to prison. I was wrong. I can't do this. Fuck it all. I hate this stupid planet. I'm done."

ABOUT THE AUTHOR

Leo X. Robertson is a Scottish process engineer, writer and filmmaker, currently living in Stavanger, Norway. He has work published by Year's Best Hardcore Horror, Best of British Science Fiction and Flame Tree Publishing, among others. Be on the lookout for his feature films The TrutherNet Apocalypse and Burnt Portraits, hopefully available later this year!

AFTERWORD

Before championed by the wonderful Matt Clarke of *Planet Bizarro Press*, the book you have just read—thank you so much for doing so! Hope you enjoyed—sat on my hard drive for maybe four years? And it wasn't one I had intended to write in the first place. I (still) have an unpublished novel called *Italo!*, a fictionalised account of the rise and fall of Italo disco, a musical genre I happen to love. I thought it might fit with *Eraserhead Press* so I contacted them. They said it sounded cool but they typically introduced authors to their press through novellas. Could I write something shorter for them? I wrote *Jesus of Scumburg*, loosely based on the life of GG Allin. They quite liked it but wanted to see something else. This book later got picked up by *Hindered Souls Press,* which promptly folded, so luckily it was acquired by *NihilismRevised*, which I think have also closed now? One of its other authors implied that to me recently, and I haven't had time to look into it.

Back to *Eraserhead Press:* for them, I wrote *Dinosaurs of the CyberVatican*. (J.L. Rojas is my husband, Juan, who loves Dan Brown and *Jurassic Park*—though he is not a fan of how I combined them!) Again they liked the style, and said it was closer to what they publish, but they had had enough of religious allusions. Fine, so I wrote *Everybody Wants to Save Supermammal City* and sent them that. By this point I was pretty sure I knew what was coming, so I also wrote *Koalita, Mon Amour* just in case. Except I stopped hearing back from *Eraserhead Press* and felt a little embarrassed pursuing them so often with so many manuscripts about which they were ambivalent. So I just stopped following up and went and wrote other stuff. If you enjoyed this book, it's a success story for *Planet Bizarro Press*, a much-needed new force on the scene that publishes books like this for which there are too few outlets. Please continue to support this awesome new publisher, and consider following me for more guaranteed weirdness in the immediate future!

Leo X. Robertson
10/03/22

NEW AND UPCOMING FROM PLANET BIZARRO

Peculiar Monstrosities - *A bizarro monster-themed anthology*
Extremely Bizarre - *An extreme horror-bizarro anthology*
Sons of Sorrow *by Matthew A. Clarke*
Porn Land *by Kevin Shamel*
Weird Fauna of the Multiverse *by Leo X. Robertson*
A Quaint New England Town *by Gregory L. Norris*
Dead Monkey Rum *by Robert Guffey*
Dad Jokes *by Justin Hunter*
Russells in Time *by Kevin Shamel*
Songs About My Father's Crotch *by Dustin Reade*
The Secret Sex Lives of Ghosts *by Dustin Reade*
Selleck's 'Stache is Missing! *by Charles Chadwick*
The Falling Crystal Palace *by Carl Fuerst*
Shithole USA *by Mark Zirbel*
DEAD HARD *by Matthew A. Clarke*

CPSIA information can be obtained
at www.ICGtesting.com
Printed in the USA
LVHW091315060522
718035LV00013B/406